"It's not as if you really have anything to hide."

Blaze looked at her.

Livi burst into laughter. "Did I really just say that?"

He chuckled. "Yeah, you did."

Their gazes locked and both of them could see the attraction mirrored in the other's eyes.

The smoldering flame Livi saw in his eyes startled her. She was by no means blind to his attraction.

Blaze pulled her into his arms. "Livi, there is something that I've wanted to do all evening." The prolonged anticipation of kissing her had become unbearable. His mouth covered hers hungrily.

Raising his mouth from hers, Blaze gazed lovingly into her eyes.

Livi drew his face to hers in a renewed embrace. Her body ached for his touch.

He kissed her again, lingering, savoring every moment.

"What are we doing?" Blaze whispered.

Livi's emotions whirled. Blood pounded in her brain, leaped from her heart and made her knees tremble. "This is something we both want," she said huskily. "We can have this one night."

Books by Jacquelin Thomas

Harlequin Kimani Romance

The Pastor's Woman
Teach Me Tonight
Chocolate Goodies
You and I
Case of Desire
Five Star Attraction
Five Star Temptation
Legal Attraction
Five Star Romance

JACQUELIN THOMAS

is a bestselling author of more than forty-five titles. Writing is still her passion, and she is currently at work on the next installment of the Alexander family series.

FIVE STAR ROMANCE

JACQUELIN THOMAS

HARLEQUIN® KIMANI™ ROMANCE

To my ever-wonderful husband,
who also happens to be my best friend.
I adore you and I'm so blessed to have been your wife for twenty-two years. My life with you continues to be first-class and a five star romance!

ISBN-13: 978-0-373-86296-2

FIVE STAR ROMANCE

For questions and comments about the quality of this book, please contact us at CustomerService@Harlequin.com.

HARLEQUIN®
www.Harlequin.com

Printed in U.S.A.

Dear Reader,

Have you ever done something that you immediately regretted? I have, and for a brief moment I wished to have the ability to rewind the clock. In *Five Star Romance,* Blaze Alexander feels exactly the same way after a weekend in Las Vegas. However, he soon discovers that what happens in Vegas does not always stay in Vegas. Blaze and Livi Carlyle are made for each other, although it takes some time for them to realize that what they share is truly a five star romance.

When two people are meant to be together, not even time can keep them apart. I hope that you will experience the thrill of their unconventional reunion and cheer for them as they forge their way to happily ever after.

Thanks so much for your support!

Best,

Jacquelin

Chapter 1

Blaze Alexander clenched his jaw in annoyance. He hated moments like these. Resentfully, he stood alongside his family as they posed for pictures at the site of the future Robert DePaul Center. Despite his personal feelings, Blaze pasted on a smile. He despised being accommodating to the press. As various cameras flashed, he silently counted down to when this would end. The family had been talking with reporters for nearly an hour.

Blaze released a soft sigh as he shifted his weight from one foot to the other. He tried to disguise his irritation in front of the representatives from the various media outlets. The corner of his mouth twisted with exasperation.

"I'm glad that's over," he whispered to Ari as the members of the media packed up and prepared to leave.

Ari was his oldest brother and the general manager of the Alexander-DePaul Hotel Group. "I don't like posing for pictures and I can't stand having my personal life played out for public entertainment. I don't know why Dad insists on having the whole family present for these events."

Ari laughed. "It doesn't matter. If he wants us there—we do as he asks. Dad never missed any of our football or basketball games. He was there for all our school programs."

Blaze reluctantly nodded in agreement. "He and Mom both put all of us before anything having to do with business."

"That's why we can't let them down," Ari stated.

"You're right. Our parents have always been there for us, especially for me," Blaze conceded. "I was the one who gave them the most grief." He winced at the memory of his teenage years.

"Well, at least we don't have to worry about you showing up on some reality TV show."

Blaze shook his head. "Never in a million years. Kellen might be another story, however. He loves attention."

"What are you two boys whispering about over here?" Sage asked as she joined them.

"Nothing important," Blaze answered, meeting his sister's gaze with a smile. Sage and Ari were near-perfect children growing up. His other siblings, Drayden, Zaire and Kellen had been mischievous in their youth, but never did any real harm. Despite his boyhood antics and troublemaking, Blaze was very close to his family.

"So what are we celebrating tonight?" Ari inquired. "This is why you and Ryan are hosting a dinner, right? We have something to celebrate?"

"We just wanted to have a nice dinner with the family," Sage responded. "That's all."

She glanced over her shoulder, then back at Ari. "I'll see you all tonight. Ryan and I need to get going. We have a lot to do before this evening."

When Sage strolled away, Ari glanced at Blaze and asked, "Do you believe her?"

"She's probably pregnant," Blaze stated matter-of-factly. "She and Ryan have been married for a couple of months now, so I wouldn't be surprised. I think they were planning to start a family right away. Look at her. She's practically floating on air."

Ari nodded in agreement.

Blaze checked his watch before walking to where his parents stood. "Hey, I have to get to a meeting, but I'll see you later tonight."

He wrapped his arms around his mother. "I love you."

"I love you, too," Barbara responded. "Thank you for coming. I know how much you hate all the attention, but it's for a good cause."

He smiled. "You know I'd do anything for you."

"I'll see you later on tonight, dear."

Blaze turned to his dad. "I need to get going, but I'll see you in the office."

"I'm not sure I'm coming in today." Malcolm awarded him a warm smile. "Your mother gently reminded me that we were supposed to spend the day together. She's planned a picnic on the beach."

Blaze noted the way his father's eyes lit up at the mention of his mother. His parents were still very much in love.

They were joined by Barbara.

Malcolm immediately took her hand in his. "I need to talk to one more person before we leave, honey. I'm all yours after that."

Blaze smiled at the look of love Barbara flashed at his father.

She kissed Malcolm on the cheek, and then announced, "I'm going to walk down to the car with Blaze."

Blaze said goodbye to his five siblings before escorting his mother down the grassy knoll toward the waiting cars.

There were still a few reporters hanging around. Probably hoping to overhear a juicy tidbit to splash all over the tabloids, Blaze thought angrily.

He had nothing against reporters except that they did not always seem to know where to draw the line when it came to reporting the news. Blaze valued his privacy, which was why he opted against living in one of the DePaul penthouse residences located in the Alexander-DePaul Hotel & Spa Resort.

At thirty-three years old, Blaze preferred not to live in what he considered the family compound. He loved his family dearly, but he did not want to have to listen to his mother's frequent suggestions that he should find a wife and settle down. He did not like disappointing her, but his mother just would not accept that Blaze had no interest in getting married. In fact, there was only one woman he could remember who held his attention. Her name was Livi and they had met a couple of years ago in Las Vegas.

The feelings she'd evoked in him during the time they'd spent together in Vegas returned from time to time. His heart ached as he hungered for Livi's presence in his life. He felt a certain warmth as the prolonged anticipation of seeing her again was almost unbearable. Blaze wanted to find Livi, but he just did not have enough concrete information about her—including her last name—to locate her.

Two years ago, Blaze had gone to Las Vegas with some of his fraternity brothers and, as fate would have it, he and Livi were staying in the same hotel. From the moment they saw each other, their mutual attraction was electric. The more he'd learned about her, the more the attraction deepened and eventually became something more.

During the brief time they'd spent together, she had mentioned that she lived in Los Angeles, but that was about it. He'd decided that her actions meant that she most likely did not want to be found.

He made a mental note to interview private detectives in the coming weeks. Blaze desperately wanted to find Livi. They had spent three fun-filled days together. Blaze hoped that their time together had meant something to her, as well.

Blaze wasn't sure when it happened, but Livi had left an imprint on his heart. It was as if she had unlocked his heart and soul, leaving his emotions as raw and erratic as a summer storm. His entire being seemed to be filled with wanting. Blaze desperately needed to see her again. If only to discover that Livi felt what they'd shared in Vegas was memorable, if fleeting.

During this time Blaze's father was notified that he was the sole heir of the late Robert DePaul's multimillion-dollar estate. When Blaze returned home from Vegas, he found out about the inheritance.

Blaze was thrilled for his parents, although he noted the mixed emotions evident on his father's face, and Malcolm's heartache at finding out that his parents had lied to him about something as important as his roots. Malcolm had grown up believing that Theodore Alexander was his father, but his mother had taken the truth to her grave.

After his wild teenage years, Blaze had vowed to be a man his father could be proud of. It was Blaze who'd stolen the car and took his friends joyriding late at night, although he did not have a driver's license. It was Blaze who'd tried to use a fake ID to buy booze. It was Blaze who'd got caught in one of the hotel rooms seducing his high school girlfriend. It was Blaze who'd chosen the wrong type of friends and ended up in jail over a home invasion and burglary—a crime he did not commit, but was arrested for along with the teens who had the stolen items in their possession.

He was what his mother called a wild child. His siblings called him the black sheep of the family, but when he glimpsed the angst on his father's face, that forever changed Blaze for the better. It was a look of hurt and disappointment.

When Malcolm found out about Robert DePaul, Blaze witnessed another strong emotion in his father—regret. Regret that he would never get to know his biological father. Seeing Malcolm in that state forced Blaze to acknowledge just how lucky he was to have parents who loved him unconditionally, despite his teenage antics, and who would always put their family first.

Chapter 2

Livi Carlyle stared at the picture located near the center of the front page of the newspaper she was reading while she waited for her friend Sybil to arrive. Sybil worked close by and they met for lunch at least once a week.

She read the article before her eyes strayed back to the picture of the Alexander family and one person in particular.

Blaze Alexander.

Livi stared at him with longing as she fantasized about being crushed in his embrace.

"Helloooo…"

The sound of Sybil's voice drew Livi out of her daydreaming. Her face flushed as she murmured, "When did you get here?"

"Just now," Sybil responded. "I could tell that you

were a million miles away from the look on your face. What were you thinking about?"

Livi quickly put away her newspaper. "Nothing."

"What have you been up to?" Sybil asked.

"Just steady working," Livi responded with a smile. "We're getting ready for the Fourth of July sale, and preparing for the fall season."

"Girl, I am loving that dress," Sybil murmured. "And those shoes."

"Thank you." Livi had on a floral-printed, V-neck dress in fuchsia, navy and green. The pewter metallic belt accentuated her tiny waist and matching sandals adorned her feet. "I found this dress when I was in New York buying for the fall season. I fell in love with it."

"I need to go on one of these buying trips of yours."

Livi chuckled.

Sybil pointed toward the newspaper sticking out of Livi's tote. "I've been reading about the new homeless shelter. I have to say that I really admire Malcolm Alexander. Building that facility is a wonderful thing to do." She took a sip of her ice water.

Livi nodded in agreement. "They're a family with strong character. In my opinion, Robert DePaul knew exactly what he was doing when he left everything to Mr. Alexander."

Sybil smiled. "So, have you and that handsome son of his run into each other yet?"

She shook her head. "I haven't seen him. He works out of the corporate offices on Wilshire Boulevard. From what I've heard, Blaze hardly comes to the hotel, and when he does, I never know about it. I hear he travels a lot."

"You have his company email address," Sybil stated.

"Why don't you send him a note? I'm sure he still remembers Vegas." She gave Livi a knowing look. "You two were inseparable."

Picking up her menu, Livi muttered, "That was a long time ago."

"It wasn't *that* long," Sybil countered. "To be honest, I don't know why you haven't said anything already. He's part of the reason you moved back to Los Angeles, so what are you waiting for?"

Livi stared at her menu as if she hadn't heard Sybil's question.

"Call the man. You keep this up and, the next thing you know, Blaze will be getting married to someone else. It will be too late then."

Sybil's words struck a chord with Livi. "I'm not calling him. What would I say?" Livi asked. "Hey, I'm the girl you partied with in Vegas. I know we haven't seen each other in two years, but I was wondering if we can get together."

Sybil chuckled. "Hey, it might work."

"I don't think so," Livi murmured. "I'll just wait until we run into each other."

"You two make such a cute couple. Who knows, maybe this is fate, and you two will end up married and living happily ever after."

Livi did not respond. Instead, she turned her attention back to the menu in her hand.

Livi felt a thread of guilt snake down her spine. She was keeping a secret from Sybil. Sybil and Amy were Livi's closest friends and the three of them shared much of their private lives. But Livi feared their judgment, so she kept mum.

After lunch, she headed back to the boutique situated on the first floor of the Alexander-DePaul Hotel & Spa Resort. Livi had completely revamped Parisian Maison into one of the premiere boutiques in the hotel industry by adding a few couture collections. The boutique used to carry mostly souvenir items designed to appeal to hotel guests who were pressed for time. Livi changed all that by adding high-end clothing and fashion accessories.

Livi had a quick meeting with her staff before retreating into her office. She sat down at her desk and opened her email.

Her heart raced at the prospect of seeing Blaze again. Maybe Sybil was right. She could write Blaze an email, but Livi could not summon up enough courage to actually send it. Initially, she was terribly angry and hurt when she thought of Blaze, but over time her anger had dissipated. She wondered how he would feel about hearing from her after all this time. Would he be angry?

Blaze was the last to arrive at the hotel for Sage and Ryan's family dinner. He had hoped to work out in his personal gym before heading to his sister's place, but got home later than he planned. Kellen and Zaire were leaving tomorrow, heading back to school in Atlanta. Blaze was not going to miss spending this evening with them.

"It's about time you got here," Sage said as she embraced him. "We've been holding dinner for you."

"I'm sorry," he responded. "You all could've started without me."

"You're here now," she stated, leading him into the dining room. "I'm surprised that you're the last one to arrive. You are always so prompt.

"Blaze is here," Sage announced. "Everyone, take your seats at the table."

He sat down next to Kellen, the youngest of the Alexander siblings. "What time are you and Zaire leaving tomorrow?"

"Around eight, I think."

"I'll be in Atlanta the first week of next month," Blaze said. "We'll all get together and do something while I'm there." Whenever he had to travel to Georgia, Blaze made sure he spent time with his younger siblings, who were in grad school.

Kellen nodded. "Cool."

Blaze glanced around the room. "Where's the little man?" he asked, referring to Joshua, Ari and Natasha's son.

"He's with my sister," Natasha responded. "She's in town for a couple of days, so they're doing dinner and a movie."

"I can't help but notice how Sage is glowing," Zaire said. "If marriage does that to you—I can't wait. You look really happy, sis."

Sage and Ryan responded in unison, "Thank you."

They looked at each other and laughed.

Blaze eyed Sage. "I don't know. I think she looks the same."

"This coming from the man who said he would never get married," Ari noted.

Blaze wiped his mouth with his napkin before saying, "Not everyone is cut out for marriage."

Ryan took a sip of water, and then said, "I wrote an article a couple of years ago on the benefits of marriage. Did you know that being married can help you beat cancer?"

"Really?" Malcolm asked.

"I did some research and found that men who have never been married had a higher mortality rate than married men," Ryan told them. "I also found that men in excellent health were about eighty-nine percent more likely to die if they were single compared to married men."

Blaze laughed.

"I read that married men live an average of ten years longer than single men," Zaire contributed.

Blaze looked at Ryan. "So you're trying to tell me that I'll die sooner than you, Dad and Ari because I don't have a wife."

"Blaze, if I were you, I'd be looking for my better half," Zaire said with a chuckle.

Sage cleared her throat loudly when everyone was almost done eating. "I know that everyone is wondering why Ryan and I wanted to have this dinner," she began. "Well, we do have some news we'd like to share." Reaching over, Sage took Ryan's hand in hers. "We're pregnant."

Everyone around the table uttered well wishes and congratulations.

"Looks like my little niece or nephew will have a playmate," Ari blurted out. "Natasha and I are also having a baby."

"What?" Zaire uttered in surprise. "Two babies."

Blaze was thrilled at the idea of becoming an uncle again. He adored Joshua.

"This is wonderful," a beaming Barbara murmured. "Two precious babies." She reached over and gave Malcolm's hand a gentle squeeze. "We're going to have two more grandchildren to spoil. Isn't that wonderful?"

Malcolm kissed her hand. "It sure is, honey."

While his parents were congratulating the expectant parents, Kellen leaned over and said in a low voice, "We're having a meeting tonight after the parents leave to discuss a surprise party to celebrate Dad's birthday."

"Okay," Blaze responded. He reached for his glass of iced tea and took a long sip.

He stole a peek at Sage. She really was glowing with happiness, prompting a smile from Blaze. Sage and Ari had both found their soul mates since moving to Los Angeles, and he was thrilled for them.

Blaze was convinced that he was destined to be a bachelor for life. He could never see himself as a family man. He was nothing like Ari or his father. Blaze enjoyed his job and it required a lot of travel. The life he had created for himself did not allow him the luxury of family.

His parents were great role models, but Blaze knew that he was not cut from the same cloth. He was devoted to his work and that left little time for anything else.

Barbara stifled a yawn as Sage and Zaire cleared away the dessert dishes.

"I guess I need to get your mother home," Malcolm announced. "She's getting sleepy."

She nodded. "Yes, I think we should head back home. It's been a long day for us both, but it's your daddy who needs his rest. He thought he could hang with some of the teens on the beach today. He played volleyball."

"I think that volleyball played me," Malcolm confessed.

They all laughed.

Barbara embraced each one of her children and then their spouses. Malcolm saluted them and grinned, and then helped Barbara gather her things. Ryan and Sage escorted them to the door. The remaining siblings gathered in the family room that was washed in a gold-and-olive-green motif. The modern furnishings were lavish, but not extravagant. Blaze and Kellen settled down on the Brazilian Cherry hardwood floor. Ari and Natasha took to the sofa along with Zaire. Drayden sat down in the overstuffed club chair.

Their parents gone, Ryan and Sage joined them and sat down on the love seat.

"I talked to Mom and she wants to have the party on their yacht," Zaire announced.

"Sounds good to me," Drayden said.

Blaze nodded in agreement. "If that's what Mom wants to do, then it's decided."

With everyone in agreement about the venue, they moved on to the event itself. They would let their mother choose the menu.

After the meeting, Blaze took the elevator down to the ground floor with Drayden.

"I hope you have a date," Drayden joked. "You seem to be in a big hurry to get out of here."

Blaze chuckled. "No, I'm just tired."

"Man, when was the last time you had a date? I haven't seen you with anyone in a while."

"I've had a few dates," Blaze responded. However, those dates progressed into nothing because he kept searching for the feeling and level of excitement he shared with Livi. "Right now my focus is on my work. There's a lot going on with the hotels, but you wouldn't know that since you chose to start your own firm."

"Don't start," Drayden said. "Mom and Dad are fine with my decision."

"I'm just giving you a hard time," Blaze said with a chuckle. "I actually respect your decision to do your own thing."

When the elevator doors opened, Blaze glimpsed a woman who reminded him of Livi, but she strolled past too quickly for him to be certain.

He cut his conversation short with Drayden and rushed out, looking for her.

"What's up?" his brother asked. "You look like you've just seen a ghost."

Blaze's eyes scanned his surroundings, but the woman was nowhere to be found.

"Bro, are you okay?"

He nodded. "Yeah. I'm fine."

Blaze made another quick sweep of their surroundings with his gaze. "I thought I saw someone I knew." When the words left his mouth, he felt a tingling sensation, the same sensation he always felt when he thought of Livi.

It was after 11:00 p.m. and Blaze preferred not to eat heavy when it was late. He made a salad and heated up a piece of grilled salmon left over from the dinner earlier with his family.

He could not stop thinking about Livi. The image of the woman near the elevator floated to the forefront of his mind.

Blaze released a long sigh. "Where are you, Livi?" he whispered.

He finished up his meal and then headed to his bedroom.

Blaze showered and changed into a pair of sweatpants and a T-shirt. He settled down in his living room to watch television, although his mind was troubled. He did not know why, but he felt anxious. Maybe it was all the media attention on his family because of the new center they were building—Blaze had no idea, but he did not like the way he was feeling.

He focused instead on his father's upcoming birthday party. Blaze was looking forward to the celebration. Malcolm certainly deserved this event, and it would serve as a token of appreciation for how much he was loved and respected.

Blaze tried to think of who he could ask to accompany him to the party. An image of Livi formed in his mind once more. Groaning in frustration, he tossed a pillow across the room.

Chapter 3

Livi laid her newspaper down on her breakfast table. The Alexander family continued to make daily headlines with the new center they were building to assist the L.A. homeless population.

Right after college, Livi had worked as Robert DePaul's assistant until he grew ill and stepped away from the business. Livi left the company shortly after his death, but returned a month ago, to take over as manager and buyer of the Parisian Maison Boutique located in the DePaul Hotel in Beverly Hills.

With Robert DePaul's son now at the reins, many of the employees decided to stay with the company. Livi had worked closely with Robert and trusted him. He was strategic in all of his decisions, so when he chose to leave everything to a son no one knew existed—Livi was not at all surprised by his actions.

As it turns out, the Alexanders were wonderful employers and astute businesspeople. Livi was thrilled that Harold DePaul was no longer at the helm. Although she liked him as a person, he was too blinded by power to take notice of anything else.

Livi often wondered what would happen when she and Blaze finally came face-to-face with each other. Would he even remember her?

Livi was not interested in his wealth. The night she met Blaze was a special one for her. Back then, Livi felt that she had met her soul mate. Everything had happened so fast.

One day, she and Blaze would have to have a conversation concerning that night because neither of them could pursue a future as long as they were bound to one another. She remembered how they were together. Being in the same city with Blaze had stirred up many emotions.

Livi pretended that she was not listening to the conversation between two of her employees as they worked to set up the display for an upcoming sale. She found that the handsome Alexander men were a constant subject of many of the female employees. She endured endless conversations from her staff and other hotel employees about Ari, Drayden and especially Blaze. Livi had heard that Drayden owned an accounting firm near Wilshire Boulevard. Like Blaze, he was rarely seen at the hotel.

Livi chuckled softly every time one of the women voiced hope that she would catch Blaze's eye. She could not be sure, but Livi did not believe that Blaze would be interested in any of them. However, she did not know that much about him. When they had met in Vegas, she had no idea that he was in any way connected to Robert DePaul. In all the years she worked with Robert, he had never shared that part of his life with her. She was stunned when she discovered that Blaze was Robert DePaul's grandson. It was indeed a small world.

Livi noticed that Blaze avoided the media as much as possible. His father and eldest brother appeared in the news frequently, but they were the face of the Alexander-DePaul Hotel Group and now the soon-to-be Robert DePaul Center.

Livi was also private and could relate to how Blaze must be feeling. Her heart ached for him, knowing how he felt about this kind of attention.

Both Sage's and Ari's marriages were featured in grocery store tabloids, and in several of the major magazines geared to the African-American market. Livi cringed at the thought of her personal life being the subject of the world's conversations and criticisms. It was another reason why she had not approached Blaze—she feared the media exposing their special connection to public scrutiny.

She and Blaze would have to be careful.

However, Livi was not sure she could wait much longer. She had to find the right time to reenter Blaze's life.

But what if there was no *right* time?

The question gnawed at her.

Livi knew that she could not keep delaying the inevitable. It only made matters worse.

Ari was working from home because he was flying out later that evening on the company jet to visit the Alexander-DePaul Hotel & Spa Resorts in Arizona. Blaze returned to the hotel the next day to meet with him.

He left his car with the valet and strolled into the spacious lobby of the hotel in Beverly Hills where Ari and Sage both maintained residences. Blaze was awestruck by the beauty of the hotel, with its Spanish Revival architecture and Mediterranean styling.

The tiny hairs on the back of his neck stood up. Blaze knew the employees were watching him. He walked briskly across the floor toward the elevators.

Whistling softly, he went up to Ari's penthouse.

The décor of his brother's home featured dark wood crown molding and soft muted color schemes of sage, plum and ivory. The five-bedroom residence offered floor-to-ceiling windows that flooded the interior with natural light.

Natasha opened the door just as he was about to knock. She stepped aside to let him enter, then said, "Don't work too hard."

He embraced her. "I should be telling you that."

She smiled. "Ari's in his office. I've ordered lunch for the two of you. It'll be delivered at noon."

"Thanks!"

Blaze walked to his brother's office.

Ari was at his desk typing something into the computer.

"I don't know who's glowing more—you or Natasha," he said with a chuckle as he took a seat. "Marriage must certainly agree with you."

Ari glanced at him and smiled. "Natasha is everything I want in a wife. Joshua is the perfect son and now we're having another baby. I'm over the moon."

"I'm thrilled for you, bro."

"What about you, Blaze? Los Angeles is filled with beautiful women—I'm surprised one of them hasn't caught your eye. You used to be quite the ladies' man."

"All my energies have been focused on work," Blaze responded. His guilt weighed upon him, choking him. He did not know how much longer his family was going to buy this explanation.

"Does Joshua know about the baby yet?" he asked.

Ari settled back in his chair. "We told him last night."

"How did he take the news?"

"I wish you could've seen him, Blaze. He walked over to Natasha and started rubbing her belly as he introduced himself to the baby. He's a proud big brother."

Two hours later, Blaze left the penthouse and took the elevator down to the lobby. His steps slowed as he neared the Parisian Maison Boutique.

Blaze stared at the woman inside talking to a couple of women carrying an armload of shopping bags. The shock of discovery hit him full force.

Her hair is much shorter now, but that woman is most definitely Livi.

Blaze hesitated, torn by conflicting emotions. What he felt for Livi cast aside any doubt as he burst through the double doors of the boutique, walking with purpose.

Livi halted, shocked, but seemed to recover quickly. "M-Mr. Alexander," she murmured. "What can I do for you?"

"Is there somewhere we can talk?" he asked, aware that everyone in the shop was watching them intently.

She gestured toward the back of the store. "Yes. My office is in the back."

Blaze gently took her arm and escorted her to the office so they could talk in private.

Once they were in the office, he closed the door behind him. "I can't believe that you've been here under my nose all this time." He came close, looking down at her intensely. "I was just about to hire a private detective to try to find you."

Her eyebrows rose in surprise. "I've only been back in Los Angeles for about a month now. I was living in San Francisco." Livi hesitated, blinking with bafflement. "Blaze, you've been looking for me?"

"I wanted to see you again." He eyed the nameplate on her desk. "So, *Carlyle* is your last name."

"Oh," she murmured. "I thought you knew that."

Blaze gave a short laugh. "I might have, but for some reason I didn't remember."

Livi smiled. "You were quite the party animal."

"So were you. But I'm sure you must have figured out that you worked for my father." Blaze paused, then added, "Livi, why didn't you let me know that you were here?"

She was completely honest in her response. "Blaze, I've only been back in Los Angeles a month. As soon as I got back, I wanted to contact you, but I didn't know what to say. I considered it many times. My friend Sybil kept telling me to call you or send an email."

"I still can't believe that you've been with the company all this time." Blaze hoped his tone concealed the mixed emotions he felt.

"Why have you been looking for me?" Livi asked.

"We had a great time in Vegas and then you disappeared. I feel like we have some unfinished business."

Livi met his gaze. "What kind of unfinished business?"

He shrugged. "That's why I've wanted to find you.

Few women have left an impression on me the way you have, Livi. We have a connection."

She smiled. "Yes, we do share a connection."

"So you feel it, too?" he asked.

Livi nodded. "Blaze..."

"I only have one regret," he quickly interjected before Livi could finish what she was about to say. "I really wish I could remember our last night together."

Livi kept her expression blank as she replayed Blaze's words in her mind.

"What do you remember about that night, Blaze?" she asked, alarmed.

"We partied and I remember our friends teasing us about spending so much time together."

Livi smiled and nodded. "They kept saying that they thought we were going to run off and elope."

Blaze laughed. "Now that would have been something."

Her eyes wandered restlessly around her office. Livi could not look him in the eye.

"Livi," Blaze prompted. "What's wrong? You've gotten quiet on me."

"Do you remember being in the hospital?"

He met her gaze. "Some of it. They said that I fell off a stage. The doctors told me that I suffered a traumatic brain injury. They said that I suffered from retrograde amnesia. I don't remember anything that happened before I fell."

"But you remember me?" Livi asked. "How is that possible?"

"According to the doctors, people with retrograde amnesia do not lose all their memories. From everything that I've read about it, usually it's the events that happened right before the injury that are lost." A smile tugged at Blaze's lips. "I could have fallen from the second floor of this hotel and I don't think I could ever forget you, Livi."

She looked up at him, meeting his warm gaze. "Every time I thought about seeing you face-to-face, I could never get past this moment. It always stopped here."

"I'm still somewhat shocked at seeing you," Blaze said. "In the back of my mind, I always felt that I would see you again, but I had no idea that it would be like this."

"I'm sorry for not coming forward sooner."

Blaze met her gaze. "That would have been nice. You owed me that much."

Hearing a noise, Livi gestured toward the door. She did not want her employees listening in on their conversation. "Blaze, can we finish this discussion at another place and time? I really have to get back out there. Martha may need some help. An employee called in sick and another one is on vacation."

"Can you meet me for lunch tomorrow?" Blaze asked.

"I'm actually hosting a baby shower for one of my employees. She's going on maternity leave in a couple of weeks."

"What about dinner?"

"I have to check my schedule, but right now I need to help Martha close up." Livi quickly wrote down her home and cell numbers. "Give me a call tomorrow and I'll let you know about dinner."

She handed the paper to Blaze.

"I'll talk to you soon," he said, then strode quickly out of the office without a glance backward.

"It was nice seeing you, too," she whispered softly. She shrugged off her disappointment, and then headed out to the sales floor.

"Are you okay?" Martha asked.

Livi nodded. "Yes, I'm fine."

Disconcerted, she crossed her arms and pointedly looked away.

"What was that all about? I've never seen Blaze Alexander in here before."

"I guess he decided to check out everything," Livi responded. "Martha, let's focus our attention on getting the shop in order. I don't want to stay late tonight."

She felt like kicking herself for not contacting Blaze. Although he had tried not to show it, Livi could tell that he was angry that she had chosen to keep her whereabouts a secret from him.

Livi had chosen to keep her heartbreak a secret from him, as well. However, that wasn't the only secret she was keeping.

Chapter 4

Blaze silently noted that Livi was more beautiful than he remembered. She looked much younger than her twenty-seven years. When they'd met in Vegas, her hair had been shoulder-length, but Livi now wore it short, the dark brown color complementing the warm glow of her sienna complexion.

His mouth tightened as he forced himself to remember the way she had treated him while they were in Vegas. Blaze left the hospital looking for her, only to discover that she had checked out of the hotel. He had heard from one of his frat brothers that Livi had come to the hospital, but she left without seeing him.

Livi's reaction to seeing him just now puzzled Blaze. She looked guilty, as if she were hiding something from him.

But what did she have to hide?

There was no point in speculation, he decided.

"Livi and I are going to sit down and have a discussion," Blaze whispered to himself. "I have to know why she ran off like that."

Strange and disquieting thoughts raced through his mind, but his heart rate increased every time he pictured Livi's smile. His first impulse had been to wrap his arms around her, but he wisely held back. He couldn't deny how much he longed to feel her in his arms or her soft lips against his. Seeing her and not being able to touch her proved to be unbearable. Blaze did not want to ignite any rumors among the hotel staff. He knew how quickly things spread along the employee grapevine. He refused to subject Livi or himself to the unwanted attentions of their coworkers.

Whatever happened in Vegas was just between Livi and him. Blaze wanted it to stay that way.

Later that evening, Livi found Sybil waiting for her when she arrived home. She was surprised by her friend's visit. She thought Sybil would be spending the evening with her fiancé.

"Hey, what are you doing here?"

Sybil had a key to Livi's condo, but she rarely used it. When she did, it was only to water Livi's plants whenever she was away on a buying trip.

"Todd and I had a fight," her friend told her. "I didn't have anywhere else to go, so I came here. I hope you don't mind." She swiped at her tear-streaked face.

"Of course I don't mind, Sybil." Livi tossed her purse on the leather ottoman, and then sank down beside her friend. "What happened this time?"

Sybil seemed to have the worst taste in men, as far as Livi was concerned. She loved her friend like a sister, but Sybil had constant drama in the relationship department.

"I think he's seeing someone else." Sybil released a long sigh. "Go ahead and say it…you told me so."

"All I'm going to say is that Todd is not worth all this heartache," Livi said. "You deserve so much better."

Sybil nodded. "I really don't want to talk about that jerk. Let's just focus on you. How are things?"

"I saw Blaze earlier," Livi announced. "He came to the boutique."

"Really?"

Livi nodded.

"What happened?"

"Nothing much," Livi answered. "We talked for a few minutes and then he left. I had to get back to work, but mostly, the boutique wasn't the right place to have that kind of discussion."

"I take it that you two will be seeing each other again then," Sybil queried.

"Blaze mentioned getting together for dinner. He was very nice to me, but that was about it, so I don't know if there is anything to talk about."

"I don't believe that. You two were very intense in Vegas."

"As the saying goes, what happens in Vegas stays in Vegas. What Blaze and I shared stayed in Vegas."

"How do you feel about it?"

Livi shrugged. "I don't know."

"I guess he turned out to be a jerk, too." Sybil rose to her feet. "I'm in need of a glass of wine. How about you?"

Livi looked up at her friend and smiled. "I have some in the fridge."

She returned with the wine bottle and a glass, which she gave to Sybil. "I wouldn't call Blaze a jerk, but he isn't the same man I met in Las Vegas."

"You're not having any?" Sybil asked, pointing to the wine.

Livi shook her head no.

They lounged on the sofa and watched a movie.

Livi stretched and yawned. "I think I'm going to call it a night. I have a long day tomorrow."

Sybil agreed as she checked her phone. "Todd's called me seven times already."

"Are you going to call him back?"

"Not tonight. I'm going to take a hot bubble bath and go to bed. I need to clear my head and I can't do that if I talk to him right now."

Livi hugged her friend. "Stay here as long as you like. I'll see you in the morning. We'll get dressed and have breakfast at the café on the corner before heading off to work."

"Sounds good," Sybil responded.

Livi showered, and then slipped into a pair of boy shorts and a camisole. She settled in bed and opened up her laptop.

She typed *retrograde amnesia* into the search engine. Livi wanted to know more about Blaze's memory loss.

The information she found confirmed what Blaze had told her. People with this condition were unable to recall events that occurred before the onset of the trauma. Her eyes filled with tears and overflowed when she read that medical research had found no way to restore the memories that had been lost.

Her heart grew sad at the thought that he would never remember their last day together.

The next evening, Livi moved around her bedroom in a panic.

She wanted to look nice for her dinner with Blaze, but she could not figure out what to wear. She glanced over at the pile of clothes on her bed.

Livi was acting as nervous as a schoolgirl going on her first date. She wanted to wear something that would rekindle what they'd experienced in Vegas.

"Sybil, I need you," she called out.

"What about that black dress with the draped ruffle down the front?" Sybil suggested as she strolled into the room. "You know, the one you bought when we were in San Diego. I'm sure it still has the tags on it."

"I thought about wearing that one, but…I don't know."

"Okay, so what time is your date?"

Livi glanced over at the clock. "In a couple of hours."

She knew style and fashion, but drew a blank at the thought of seeing Blaze tonight. Livi wanted to "wow" him.

Sybil gestured toward the closet. "C'mon, let me see what we can come up with."

Livi pulled out the black dress with the draped ruffle.

"No, it's not sexy enough," Sybil said with a shake of her head.

Livi tossed it on the bed, and then walked back to her closet.

This time she came out with a sleeveless, drop-waist, draped, red dress. A strip of gold beading adorned the shoulders. "What about this?" Livi asked, holding up the jersey knit dress.

"That's the one. It hugs your body in all the right places," Sybil stated. "Wear your black platform pumps. The ones with the gold studs."

Livi smiled and nodded. "I have the matching purse for those shoes, too."

"Are you planning on wearing any makeup?"

Livi frowned. "Do I need to?"

"Just a little," she suggested. "And wear your hair slicked back."

Sybil sat in the living room watching television while Livi showered and prepared for her date.

When Livi entered the room twenty minutes later, her friend gave her a thumbs-up.

"You look great."

"Thanks so much for your help, Sybil."

She surveyed her reflection in the wall mirror.

Livi was pleased with what she saw, and hoped that it served as a subtle reminder to Blaze of what they once shared.

They had elected to meet at the Chart House restaurant in Marina del Rey. Livi knew Blaze chose not to eat at one of the hotel restaurants because he did not want any of the hotel employees to see them having dinner together.

Livi left early for the restaurant so she could be the first to arrive. It would give her a few moments to compose herself before seeing Blaze.

The Chart House was one of her favorite places to eat. Livi loved the stunning waterfront location that offered scenic views of the marina and picturesque Southern California skies.

To her dismay, Blaze was already at the restaurant and was seated in one of the booths by the window. Livi took a deep breath as she walked over to join him.

He stood up and waited until she sat down before returning to his seat.

Livi bit back a smile. Blaze couldn't seem to take his eyes off her.

She sat in the chair, her fingers tensed in her lap.

"Thank you for meeting me here," he said, recovering.

"It sounded more like an order than an invitation," she muttered uneasily.

He seemed taken aback by her response. "I didn't mean it that way."

Livi gave a slight shrug.

The waiter approached their table.

Blaze and Livi both ordered a glass of chardonnay.

Their gazes met and held, making Livi nervous. She thought she detected a flicker in his intense eyes, causing her pulse to skitter alarmingly.

"You're staring," she murmured and stirred uneasily in her chair.

"I'm sorry," he responded. "Livi, I can't believe we're in the same room after all this time. I really thought that I would never see you again."

She picked up her menu with trembling hands. "I wanted to contact you, Blaze. I just didn't know what to say, especially after I left the way I did."

"I'd really like to know why you ran away like that," Blaze stated. "That's what I could never understand. I heard that you came to the hospital but I don't remember seeing you. What I do remember is that we clicked immediately and I thought we could talk about anything and everything. Was I mistaken?"

Awkwardly, she cleared her throat. "No, Blaze, I admit that what I did was very immature—it just seemed like a good idea at the time." Her hands, hidden from sight, twisted nervously in her lap.

The waiter came to take their dinner order.

She tried to think of a plausible explanation. "Blaze, my flight was leaving in a couple of hours. I just panicked."

"So you have no regrets about our time together?"

Livi shook her head. "I don't." She took a long sip of her ice water, and then said, "However, you can't really say the same, since you don't remember anything about our last day together."

Their food arrived.

Blaze regarded her quizzically for a moment, and then pointed toward her plate. "You're not eating."

Livi settled back in her seat. "I'm not as hungry as I thought. I'm going to take it home and eat it later." In his presence, Livi could not imagine doing something as simple as chewing. She was so nervous that she couldn't even manage normal activities.

Blaze took another bite of his steak. "This is really delicious. I'm glad you chose this place. Now that I know about it, I'll come back here often."

Livi finished off her glass of water. "I'm glad you like it."

Blaze was at ease and comfortable in her company. She wished she could be the same in his, but her secret was gnawing at her.

She studied his face for a moment, and then asked,

"What do you like to do when you're not working, Blaze?"

"I enjoy a good game of basketball," he responded. "Dancing is one of my favorite pastimes, collecting vintage car models and reading. I'm a huge mystery fan."

"We have all those things in common," Livi said. "Except for the model cars. I don't collect anything other than shoes. I love shoes."

Blaze chuckled. "I'm not surprised by that at all."

Livi grinned. "Hey, I know about your little Nike shoe habit."

He held up his hands in defense. "I'm just saying…"

Shaking her head, Livi laughed.

"Now that I know where you are, I'd definitely like to get to know you better," Blaze announced. Sitting here, talking and laughing like this, reminded him of Vegas.

Blaze eyed her for a moment before adding, "I feel as if there's something you want to say to me."

"We haven't seen each other in two years, Blaze," Livi said. "I guess I'm still in that *I can't believe that we're here together* stage."

Blaze smiled. "It really is good to see you again."

After a moment, she said, "You can't imagine how shocked I was to find that you were connected to Robert DePaul. I never thought I'd see you again. Especially since you lived in Aspen, Georgia. Although I have to admit, I considered coming to look for you."

"What made you change your mind?"

She shrugged. "I guess I wasn't sure how you would respond."

Blaze adjusted his tie. "My life changed in so many ways during that trip."

If you only knew, she wanted to add. Instead, she opened her purse and fidgeted with something.

"Blaze, do you remember my name?"

He nodded. "It's Elizabeth. I just didn't remember your last name, if you even told me, mystery woman."

They both laughed.

"What is the last thing you remember about our time together?" Livi asked.

Blaze searched his memory. "I think we were talking about going to a concert or something."

"We made plans to see Jazz Murphy perform. He's one of your frat brothers."

Blaze nodded. "Then it gets hazy after that."

His gaze traveled over her face seductively. "I really wish I could remember that last day. I feel as if I'm missing something important. All I know is what happened at the concert. My frat brothers told me that Jazz invited us up to the stage."

Livi nodded. "You all did a step routine and the next thing I know you were falling off the stage." She shuddered at the memory.

"You were there?"

"Yes," she responded. "We were there together. On that last day, we met for breakfast. Afterward, we went to the Stratosphere Tower."

"So we actually went there," Blaze murmured. "We had discussed going to the observation deck the day we met."

Puzzled, Livi nodded. "I'm not afraid of heights, but that deck was so high that we had an eye-level view of the helicopters." She gazed at Blaze. "You don't remember, do you?"

He shook his head. "I wish I could."

"You told me about your parents and how they met," Livi said. "They met at the county fair. Your father saw your mother and kept following her around until she confronted him. She told him that he might as well invite her to ride with him on the Ferris wheel. He did, although he was afraid of getting on the ride."

Blaze nodded and smiled. "That was the first and last time he ever got on any ride. He was so sick afterward. My mother said it was my dad's determination to move past his fear of heights to win her affection that attracted her initially. They married a few months later and are still going strong thirty-eight years later."

The air around them seemed electrified, which only added to Blaze's discomfort. Her memory of what happened gave Livi power.

"How long have you worked at the hotel?" he asked after a moment. "If I remember correctly, you told me you were an executive assistant at the time."

"I was," Livi responded. "I was actually your grandfather's assistant."

"So you knew Robert DePaul pretty well then."

It was more of a statement than a question.

Livi nodded. "I knew him as well as anyone could outside of his family. Robert was a good man…a very savvy and intelligent businessman. Your father reminds me of him a great deal."

"I would have liked to have met him," Blaze confessed. "I understand why he waited, but I think that it bothers my dad—the way all this came about. Robert was a complete stranger to us all."

"I'm sure Harold hasn't made it any easier for your family."

"Hopefully he's too busy with the expansion of the Blythewood Hotels to try to sabotage us."

"Your father can handle Harold."

Blaze nodded in agreement. "I understand why Harold's upset, but to go after my family the way he has—it's not acceptable."

"I'm pretty sure you've seen the last of Harold," Livi said. "You've beaten him at every turn, from what I've heard. I don't think he'll bother coming after you again."

"As much as I'd like to believe that, I'm not so sure," Blaze said. "I'm sure the man is trying to find something on my family. We're not worried, though. We don't have anything to hide."

Chapter 5

Livi felt an electrifying jolt of shock run through her as she silently contemplated what could happen. What if someone decided to look into Blaze's past—or hers, for that matter?

"You okay?" Blaze asked, apparently noting her sudden discomfort.

A new and unexpected warmth surged through her, emanating from the way Blaze was looking at her, his eyes caressing her softly.

She struggled to keep from blurting out her news. Now was definitely not the right time or place.

"I was thinking about all the stuff you told me about your childhood and adolescence," Livi stated. "You and I have so much in common. I was rebellious in my teen years, as well. I don't know if you remember my telling you that.... Anyway, when I see you now, it's hard for me to believe you were ever the kid you described."

Blaze chuckled. "Oh, I was definitely that person. But you…" He shook his head. "What did you do that was so rebellious?"

"I used to sneak out of my parents' house and take the car."

He shook his head in disbelief.

"I did," Livi said. "I was a handful. I'm sure our parents are thrilled that we're finally past our teenage years—I know my parents couldn't be happier."

Laughing, Blaze nodded in agreement. "Do you think that's why we were so drawn to each other? Because we're both rebels?"

"That's probably part of it," Livi responded. "I was also attracted to your mind. We had some great conversations on politics, education and life in general."

"I do remember some of those conversations," Blaze stated with a grin. "A couple of them got really heated."

Livi smiled. "You and I have a difference of opinion when it comes to education in low-income areas."

"We won't rehash that conversation," he said. "I would rather spend the evening talking about the good times we had in Vegas."

"We definitely had those," she murmured in a low voice. Livi implored him with her eyes to try to remember.

Blaze was still drawn to Livi.

He enjoyed listening to her as she discussed her plans for the future during dinner. He admired her determination and optimism.

In the back of his mind, Blaze briefly considered that Livi's renewed interest in him could be financial, but he forced that thought out of his mind. He had never thought of Livi as a gold digger, but then Blaze never thought she was the type of woman to run away from any situation.

While he still found her irresistible, he vowed not to be led by his heart. Things had changed for him since that time in Vegas.

Livi had gotten under his skin in a huge way, but she'd left when Blaze had needed her most.

Blaze shook his head as if to ward off the thought. He did not even want to admit it to himself. Pain of any kind was a sign of weakness as far as he was concerned.

"Blaze…" Livi prompted. "What are you thinking about?"

"Why didn't you come see me when you came to the hospital? Why did you just leave like that?"

She met his gaze. "I didn't want to intrude. When you fell off that stage, I tried to get to you, but security wouldn't let me. By the time I made it to the front, the paramedics were rushing you to the hospital."

"You didn't ride with me?" he asked.

Livi shook her head no. "I could hardly get any information on your condition from your friends. They were very protective of you."

"I didn't know, Livi. All they told me was that you had stopped by the hospital and then left."

"I felt as if I wasn't wanted there."

"I was in and out of consciousness that night."

"I realize that, but back then, I didn't know," Livi said. "I made a wrong assumption. I see that now."

"I guess I can understand why you would be so hesitant to contact me then." Blaze checked his watch. "It's getting late and I have a long day tomorrow."

Livi stood up. "Thanks for dinner."

"It was my pleasure."

Blaze escorted Livi to her car outside the restaurant.

He surprised them both by giving her a chaste kiss on the lips.

A quiver surged through Livi's veins. She waited for her quickened pulse to return to normal.

She was both surprised and pleased by Blaze's kiss.

"I...I don't really know why I just did that. It just seemed natural."

She smiled. "I didn't mind. I'm just surprised because you seemed angry with me earlier."

"There is a part of me that's angry," Blaze admitted. "I didn't like the way you just up and left me, but I'll be okay."

"Thank you for dinner," she murmured. "I enjoyed sitting down with you and talking."

"It's going to take some time," Blaze responded.

"If I had a chance to do it all over again, I would handle everything differently."

He gave her a brief hug. "At least now, we have a chance to renew our friendship."

Chapter 6

"William is not doing well," Meredith DePaul announced. "You really should go by and visit your brother."

"You and William have always been close. I'm sure he'll get better if I'm not around. The last thing I want to do is cause him to have a setback," Harold DePaul said.

"He loves you and so do I, Harold."

"Yet, you two chose to join the Alexanders in their quest to take everything away from the DePaul family."

"Harold, when are you going to put an end to this feud between you and Malcolm's family?"

He glanced at his sister from his desk. "Meredith, I'm not interested in rehashing this argument."

She paced back and forth across the carpeted floor in his office. "I'm not trying to argue with you. I just want you to stop this nonsense. Malcolm and his family are good people. They are a part of our family, Harold. Uncle Robert would not want us to have this gulf between us. He would want the family to come together."

Harold's telephone rang.

"I need to take this call," Harold told his sister. "We're still on for lunch tomorrow, right?"

Meredith sighed in resignation. "Sure. I'll see you then."

She sent him a sharp look before walking out of his office.

He answered his cell phone. "Yes…?"

"Harold DePaul, I am about to make your day."

He frowned. "Who is this?"

"George Pepper. I did some work for you last year."

"George, what is it you have for me?"

He chuckled. "Oh, no, it's not going to be so simple. You see, what I have for you is going to cost you plenty."

"I don't think so," Harold responded coolly.

"I will tell you this much—the Alexanders have secrets and I've uncovered one of them. Trust me, this one is huge."

Harold was silent on the other end.

"You still there?" George inquired.

"Come to my office this afternoon," Harold said. "Around three. And, George, this had better be worth my time."

Harold thumbed his fingers on his desk.

George had definitely sparked his curiosity. Harold did not hold out much hope because the detectives he had hired to look into the Alexander family had not turned up so much as a speeding ticket.

He would hear the man out, but Harold considered

his conversation with his sister. Perhaps Meredith was right. It was time to move on.

Livi slowly turned the doorknob and opened her door. She stepped into her spacious bedroom. At the far end of the room, a floor-to-ceiling window gave Livi a view of much of Los Angeles.

She crossed the varnished hardwood floor in bare feet, walking toward the platinum bed that framed a purple-and-teal-colored comforter and several pillows. Livi sat down on her bed and reclined against the stack of pillows leaning against the king-size headboard.

From the moment she realized that Blaze was within arm's reach, Livi bounced back and forth between yearning for him and keeping her distance. She was experiencing a gamut of emotions. One of them was guilt.

I'm a coward.

She should have sought him out from the very beginning, instead of letting so much time go by. Livi had been afraid and kept putting it off. Now, she was afraid that it was too late.

Too late for what? What did she want from Blaze?

Livi wanted to know if what she had felt back then with him was real. It was something that had plagued her thoughts and her heart from the time she left him. From the moment they met, the very air around Livi had seemed electrified. She had found in him a kinship through their shared interests. She and Blaze both had a heart for service to the community. They both loved sports and were avid readers.

She recalled a memory of Blaze pausing to pick up a little girl who had fallen down. He made sure that she was safe with her mother before walking away. He cared about others. She noted that he was also a generous man, always tipping over and above what was required.

He was also romantic. Blaze arranged to have her favorite chocolates waiting in her hotel room the night of their first date. The next morning a half a dozen roses greeted her. When Blaze found out that she had missed her prom because she had injured her foot during a high school basketball game, he re-created her prom night for their second date. It was then that Livi had fallen in love with him.

She had thought she could leave the memories and the emotions behind.

Livi climbed off her bed and strode back over to the window, allowing her gaze to drift over the moonlit sky as she relived her time with Blaze.

What is wrong with me?

They had spent three days together. *Three days.*

The spring weather still held a trace of briskness, prompting Livi to rub her arms to ward off the chill. Livi continued standing at the window, listening to the steady rhythm of the Los Angeles nightlife below, while contemplating her future.

Livi wanted to explore a future with Blaze. He possessed all the qualities she wanted in a man. Trust and honesty were extremely important to Blaze. It was the same for her. No relationship could work without them.

"I don't want to lose him," she whispered to the empty room.

"What is this about?" Harold demanded as soon as George Pepper strolled into his office, looking smug and overconfident. The aging detective had on a pair of loose pants that had seen better days and a wrinkled shirt with flowers all over it.

"As I explained on the phone, I have some information about the Alexander family that you will find very useful."

"I doubt that," Harold retorted. "It seems my *cousins* are law-abiding citizens with bleeding hearts." He was positive that whatever George thought he had discovered could not be worth anything.

"I've never known you to give up quite so easily."

"Sometimes, you just have to walk away."

George leaned back in his chair. "I think you're going to have a change of heart once you hear what I have to say."

Chapter 7

The next day, Livi spotted Blaze in the hotel with a little boy. She surmised that the child was Ari and Natasha's son. Although she had not seen Joshua in a long time, Livi had heard that Joshua's cancer was gone and the little boy was doing well.

Blaze saw her and waved.

Livi felt an eager affection coming from Blaze when he and Joshua entered the boutique. He looked her over seductively.

She pretended not to notice as a vaguely sensuous frisson passed between them, but every time his gaze met hers, Livi's heart turned over in response.

"Well, who is this handsome young man?" Livi asked, a smile tugging at her lips.

"I'm Joshua."

"This is my nephew," Blaze said. "He's Ari and Natasha's son."

Livi bent down. "I know you don't remember me, but I used to babysit you when your mommy had to travel. You were about three years old and you used to love to come to my house."

"Do you have a puppy?"

"I did," Livi confirmed. "You remember Spottie?"

Joshua nodded. "Do you still have him?"

Livi shook her head no. "He's not a little puppy anymore, so he lives with my parents now. They have a huge yard for him to run and play in. I visit him as much as I can, though."

"He used to take naps with me."

Laughing, Livi nodded. "He sure did."

"Joshua, why don't you look around for that birthday present for your mom," Blaze suggested.

"Okay."

Joshua rushed over to a table display of scarves.

"Are you two doing some male bonding this afternoon?" Livi inquired.

Blaze grinned and nodded.

"Look, Uncle B," the little boy called out. "Mommy would like this scarf. It's the perfect gift for her birthday."

"Joshua certainly has good taste."

Blaze agreed. "Definitely."

"Can I get this for her?" asked Joshua.

Blaze nodded. "You sure can."

"You two seem very close," Livi commented with a smile.

"We are," Blaze confirmed.

After Joshua made his purchase, Livi noted that Blaze did not seem in any hurry to leave.

"Did you need something?" she asked after a short pause. "You never come into the boutique."

"I can't pretend I don't know you," he said in a low voice. "I was here at the hotel, so I came by to say hello."

"Oh, okay," she responded.

He broke into a wide grin. "Hello."

Livi chuckled. "Hello to you, too."

"I sense that there's still some tension between us," Blaze said. "Livi, I don't want that. To be honest, I'm hoping we can be friends."

Livi felt a warm glow flow through her. "You want to be friends?"

"Yes," Blaze responded. "Is that so surprising?"

"No. Actually, I'm glad you feel that way. I'd like nothing more than to be your friend."

Livi greeted a woman who had just entered the boutique. "I'd better get back to work. Joshua, your mother is going to love her gift from you."

"I know," the little boy responded. "Mommy loves scarves. Uncle B, you should get her one, too."

Livi bit back a smile as Blaze responded, "I have a gift for her already. It's not as nice as this, but I think she'll like it."

He glanced at Livi and said, "I'll see you later."

Livi's friend Amy strolled into the boutique just as Blaze and Joshua were leaving. She glanced over her shoulder. "Was that…"

Livi nodded. "It was Blaze," she confirmed.

Amy followed her into her office and closed the door. "When did all this happen?"

"What are you talking about?" Livi asked as she sat

down at her desk. "He just came in with his nephew to buy a gift."

Amy dropped down into one of the chairs facing her. "How long have you two—"

Livi interrupted her by saying, "We reconnected a few days ago."

"And?" Amy prompted with a smile.

"And nothing," Livi responded matter-of-factly.

"I'm shocked."

"Why?" Livi asked. "We haven't seen each other in almost two years. Blaze and I are just getting reacquainted. That's all."

"Who would have imagined that a man you met one night in Vegas would turn out to be none other than Robert DePaul's grandson?" Amy commented. "How ironic is that?"

"I never would have imagined it. Amy, I was shocked beyond words when I found out."

"You still have feelings for him?"

Livi nodded. "I do. It's crazy, but every time we are in the same room, I just feel tingly." She broke into a short laugh. "I sound like a schoolgirl in love for the first time."

Amy laughed. "Yeah, you do. I think it's pretty sweet."

"I wonder if he feels the same way," Livi said. "Blaze hasn't said all that much about how he feels about me."

"Has he asked you out?"

Livi shook her head. "He did say that he wanted us to be friends. Maybe that's all he's looking for right now."

"Is that enough for you?" Amy asked.

"It'll have to be," Livi responded. "This will give us a chance to get to know each other."

Amy rose to her feet. “I came by here to see if you wanted to have lunch, but then I got sidetracked when I saw Blaze.”

“Do you still want to grab lunch?” Livi asked.

“Sure.”

Livi pushed away from her desk and stood up. “Let’s go. I’m starving.”

Blaze enjoyed a nice lunch with Joshua before returning to the hotel where they took the private elevator to Ari’s residence.

“Can I spend the night with you on Saturday?” Joshua asked.

“Sure, if it’s all right with your parents. You’re welcome to hang out with me anytime you want.”

Joshua grinned. “We can eat burgers and play video games.”

“And read some books and finish that science project that’s due next week,” Blaze responded.

“Awww…”

“Hey, buddy…schoolwork before fun, right?”

“I guess,” Joshua mumbled.

When they walked into the penthouse, they found Franklin there with Ari. Franklin was now head of security, but he’d worked as Robert DePaul’s butler. Malcolm and his family decided they had no use for a butler, but with Franklin’s military background, he could oversee the security team for the hotel group.

“Daddy, I have a gift for Mommy. Uncle B helped me pick it out.” Joshua showed Ari the scarf.

“Very nice.”

Franklin prepared to leave the two brothers alone, but Blaze stopped him. “I need to speak with you.”

Blaze excused himself from Ari and walked with Franklin to the living room so that they could talk in private. He knew that he could trust the man who had once served Robert and now his family.

"Franklin, I need to ask for a favor."

"What is it?"

"Livi Carlyle. What do you know about her?"

Franklin's expression never changed as he settled down in one of the wingchairs. "May I ask why?"

Blaze sat down on the sofa. He was not sure how to explain it, but decided to be truthful. "A couple of years ago, Livi and I met in Vegas. We spent some time together."

"She went to celebrate her birthday with some friends," Franklin contributed. "I remember because she brought me back a souvenir. She also told me about a young man she met there. Livi never mentioned a name, though."

"As you may have already guessed, we recently reconnected. I really like her, Franklin."

"She worked for Robert as his assistant, straight out of college. Livi is a nice girl and she comes from a solid family. She's a hard worker and she's honest."

"That's exactly what I thought, but I wanted to be sure," Blaze said. "I just wanted to make sure there were no hidden motives."

"I don't believe you have to worry about that with Livi," Franklin stated.

Blaze smiled. "I'm glad to hear it because I like her a lot. I'm thinking about dating her."

"I don't believe you can go wrong with Livi."

"Thanks, Franklin. I appreciate your candor."

"Livi is not the kind of girl to…she wants a husband and a family," Franklin said. He rose to his feet.

"I'll keep that in mind," Blaze responded.

At home, Blaze picked up the phone and dialed Livi's number. "Hey, it's me," he said when she answered on the third ring.

"Hey you," Livi responded.

"Are you busy?"

"No, I was just sitting here trying to decide what I wanted to do about dinner."

"I haven't eaten, so why don't we pick a restaurant and have a meal together?" Blaze suggested.

"Sounds great to me," Livi responded. "What type of food are you in the mood for?"

"How about Mexican? There's this great little place right here on Wilshire. It's called La Parrilla."

"I've heard of it," she said. "I know exactly where it is. I'll meet you there."

"Does seven o'clock work for you?" he asked.

"Yes. I'll see you then."

He hung up the phone and headed straight to the shower.

Thirty minutes later, he got to the restaurant.

Livi had just arrived when he pulled into the parking lot. Blaze parked beside her and got out.

They stood in silence for a moment.

"I really wanted to see you," Blaze said. His feelings for Livi had nothing to do with reason. Her gaze wrapped around him like a warm blanket.

"Same here," Livi responded with a tender smile.

He took her by the hand and led her into the restaurant. They were both smiling.

Blaze pulled out a chair for Livi, and then took the seat across from her.

"Have you eaten here before?" she asked him.

"A couple of times. I've liked everything I've tried."

Livi picked up the menu, scanning it slowly. "I'm going to have the shrimp fajitas."

"I think I'll have the same thing," Blaze announced.

The waiter arrived with glasses of water, chips and salsa.

Blaze gave their orders and he disappeared as quickly as he had come.

"You look the same," he told Livi. "You're still as beautiful as ever."

"Thank you for the compliment. I'll take it."

"What made you decide to cut your hair?"

"I wanted to do something different," Livi responded. "You don't like it short?"

"Actually, I do," Blaze said. "I'm not a hair fanatic. As long as it looks good, I'm okay with it long, short or whatever." He paused a moment before continuing, "I have this event coming up and I'd like for you to be my date to the St. Mark Charity Gala."

"What do you think people will say when I'm seen with you?" Livi wanted to know.

"The focus is more on my dad and Ari during these types of events," Blaze answered. "I don't think we have anything to worry about."

"Blaze, are you sure about this?" Livi was worried that the media would suddenly take an interest in their friendship.

He nodded. "Yes. I want you to be my date for the gala."

"I can't believe that I'm actually considering this," Livi said after a slight pause.

"I want to get to know you better..."

"Blaze, I'm not sure this is such a good idea," she said. "I think people are more inclined to ask questions if I just show up at the gala with you out of the blue."

He considered that, and then said, "I still want you to be my date for the gala, but I understand what you're saying. You don't have to worry. I don't have any secrets for anyone to uncover. We are two friends attending a charity event together.

"It would give us a chance to get to know one another," Blaze said. "Are you okay with getting to know the real me?"

Livi nodded. "Actually, I'd like that."

Blaze smiled. "Then it's settled. You're my date for the charity event."

The waiter returned with their food.

"How did Natasha like Joshua's gift?" Livi asked.

"She loved it. I think mostly because it was from him. Joshua is a great little kid."

"You sound like a proud uncle." She wiped her mouth on the cloth napkin.

"That's because I am," he confirmed.

Blaze took a sip of his water. "I am going to be the uncle who spoils his nieces and nephews like crazy."

"Do you want children one day?"

"I think it would be pretty cool to be a dad, but...I don't know if it's in the cards for me. I already told you some of the stuff I did. That stuff haunts you."

Livi settled back in her chair. "Blaze, you were a typical teenage boy. I don't think you should be so hard on yourself. If anything, your experiences will probably shape the type of father you will be."

"I don't know what I'd do if a child of mine started running around with the wrong crowd and got into trouble. I'd probably respond the same way my dad did. When I got arrested, he made me stay in jail for the night." Blaze gave a tiny smile. "That was enough for me to realize that that is a place I never want to see again."

"He did the right thing by letting you stay in jail," Livi stated. "I would have done the same thing."

Blaze agreed. "What about you? Do you want to be a mother?"

Livi nodded. "I'm looking forward to motherhood." She paused for a moment and then said, "We never imagined our meeting turning out like this."

Blaze agreed, "It's kind of surreal."

"I admire the way you and your family have held up during all of Harold's manipulations. I've known him a long time, but I was surprised by some of what I'd heard he was doing. He used to be a pretty decent guy."

"I just want him to leave my family alone. As long as he stays out of our affairs, we're cool."

After dinner, Blaze walked Livi out to her car. "Thank you for having dinner with me."

"It was my pleasure," she murmured.

He planted a kiss on her lips the same way as before.

Livi swallowed her disappointment at the chaste kiss Blaze gave her. Even in remembrance, she felt the intimacy of the way he used to kiss her.

Blaze was just as disappointed. He wanted to kiss

her deeply, but held back because he thought it might be too soon. He wanted to take their relationship one day at a time.

Chapter 8

Livi exhaled a long sigh of contentment as she settled down on her sofa.

"I guess dinner with Blaze went pretty well," Sybil said, as she stood in the doorway leading from the living room to the dining room.

"We had a lovely time," Livi said with a grin. "It reminded me of our time in Vegas."

Sybil joined her on the sofa. "I'm glad to see you so happy."

"Blaze asked me out on a date," Livi announced.

"That's great."

"We're going to the St. Mark charity event."

"I guess we need to get busy shopping for your gown."

Livi nodded. "It has to be perfect."

"It will be," Sybil responded with a smile. "My relationship is crappy right now, but we are going to make sure you get your man."

Livi's smile disappeared. "So things aren't any better?"

Sybil shook her head. "He is still lying about cheating, but I have proof. Cell phone records don't lie."

"I'm so sorry."

"We're not focusing on me right now. Livi, the first time I saw Blaze, I just knew that he was the man for you. I want you to be happy."

Livi hugged her friend. "I want the same for you."

"My time will come," Sybil said. "I'm not worried about me."

"What did you do for dinner?" Livi inquired.

"Amy and I grabbed a meal."

"Good," Livi said. "I'm glad to see that you're getting your appetite back." She was worried about Sybil because she had not been eating much since her breakup with Todd.

"I've got to go on with my life and that's what I intend to do." Sybil stood up and then reached down to pull up Livi. "C'mon, let's get on the computer and see what we can find for you to wear to the charity gala."

It touched her that Sybil put aside her personal angst to help her find the perfect dress for her date with Blaze. She made a mental note to set up a day of pampering for Sybil at the hotel.

"How are things going?" Natasha asked Livi when she entered the boutique the following day.

"Great," Livi responded as the two women embraced. "I'm so glad you're back in Los Angeles."

Livi smiled. "It's really good to be back. Hey, I saw

Joshua the other day and I can't believe how big he's gotten."

Lowering her voice, Natasha said, "He's also going to be a big brother. I'm going to have another baby."

The two women embraced a second time.

"I'm so happy for you."

They walked back to Livi's office and sat down to catch up.

"So when I saw you in San Francisco two years ago, you acted as if you could hardly stand Ari. What changed?"

"From the moment I met Ari, I admired his work ethic and his determination. But the more I got to know him on a personal level, the more I fell in love with him."

"I've heard that he and his father are a lot like Robert," Livi said.

Natasha nodded. "They share many of Robert's qualities. I suppose it's in their blood. You know Robert has been in the hotel business since he was old enough to carry luggage. Malcolm has pretty much the same background. His family has managed a couple of hotels in Georgia for several generations. Robert met Malcolm's mother when he opened the hotel in Wilmington, North Carolina. She worked there as a housekeeper."

"Robert never shared that part of his life with me," Livi said. "I always felt that he was harboring regret over something, but I had no idea what it could be."

"I wished that he could have gotten to know Ari and my father-in-law. Robert talked a lot about Malcolm's mother during the last few months of his life. Letting her leave with his child was the hardest decision he had ever made, according to Robert."

"It sounds as if he really loved her."

Natasha nodded. "He did, Livi. Robert went to the hospital to see her right before she died. He flew to be by her side as soon as he heard she was sick."

"Really?"

"Yes. Robert even went to the cemetery to say his final farewell. He waited until her family left, though. He loved her until the very end."

"Maybe they are finally together," Livi murmured. "I'd like to believe that a love like that can survive anything, even death."

Natasha broke into a grin. "You have always been a romantic, Livi."

"I believe in love…what can I say?"

"So have you met anyone special?" Natasha inquired.

Livi shook her head no. "I haven't really been looking. Work has kept me pretty busy." She wasn't sure that she should mention that she and Blaze had a past, so Livi kept quiet.

"I have a couple of single brothers-in-law," she said with a smile. "I could introduce you. I think you and Drayden would make a cute couple."

She shook her head no. "Definitely not, Natasha."

Frowning, Natasha asked, "Why not? What's wrong with Drayden?"

"I'm sure he's okay, but he's not my type."

Natasha gave her a knowing grin. "Oh, I see. Blaze is more your type."

Livi did not respond.

Natasha chuckled. "I'm right."

"It doesn't matter," Livi stated. "I'm sure Blaze will find the woman of his dreams on his own. He seems to be a very capable man."

Natasha backed off. "Okay, I won't try to set you up with one of my brothers-in-law."

"Thank you, Natasha. If I'm supposed to be with an Alexander man, I want him to come looking for me."

Their conversation came to a halt when William De-Paul knocked on the open door.

Livi rose to her feet and walked over to embrace the man. He seemed older than he was because he had been plagued by heart attacks and a stroke. "How are you?" she asked.

"I'm doing fine."

William DePaul, Harold's brother, retired shortly after his uncle died. William often came to the hotel for lunch or dinner. He and Malcolm seemed to get along well and kept in constant contact.

He and Natasha talked for a moment before she left the boutique.

William had come to purchase a bracelet for his daughter. Livi showed him what they had to offer.

"I know she said it was a sapphire and white gold bracelet," he was saying.

"Oh, I know which one she's talking about," Livi responded. "Here it is."

He looked it over and smiled. "I'll take it."

Livi had one of her employees ring up the purchase.

"I'm glad you decided to come back home," William said with a smile.

"Me, too."

"Ari treating you well?"

Livi nodded. "He and his father are wonderful to work for."

"Uncle Robert knew what he was doing," William stated. "Too bad my brother hasn't accepted that."

"It may take some time, but he will," Livi said. "Harold doesn't have a choice."

There were times when Blaze missed his hometown. In Aspen, there were no hour-long commutes to work in a sea of heavy traffic, no outrageously priced real estate markets, no driving all the way across town to reach his favorite stores or restaurants. The residents all knew one another.

At home at last, he kicked off his shoes and removed his tie. He just wanted to relax for a moment before working out.

Blaze headed to the refrigerator and pulled out a bottle of water that was decorated with Swarovski crystals.

Bling H2O.

He laughed. He still couldn't get over the idea of designer water. The hotel kept the brand in stock for high-profile guests with discriminating tastes. Ari called it the Cristal of bottled water. In addition to Bling H20, the hotel also kept King Island Cloud Juice stocked for select VIP guests.

Water was water in Blaze's opinion.

He finished off his water and then changed into workout clothes.

An image of Livi formed in his mind. He wished that he could remember every single moment in Vegas with her. How could he forget what must have been a beautiful time?

Blaze shook his head sadly. He wanted his memories back.

Blaze never told anyone about his trip to Vegas. He knew his parents would have been disappointed in his behavior—partying irresponsibly with his frat brothers. Out of all the Alexander siblings, Blaze had been the most stubborn and difficult.

Chapter 9

Harold strolled around the newly opened Rosen Hotel Hollywood, a premier, ultraluxury property that was part of the Wilmington Group. It was nothing like the Alexander-DePaul chain of hotels. They could not come close. The Blythewood Hotel chain was proud of its new property in Hollywood and hoped Harold could make the Rosen as successful as its competitors—the properties under Malcolm's control.

He walked to his office and grabbed his car keys. There was someone he needed to see.

"Harold, what are you doing here?" Livi asked when he walked into the boutique twenty minutes later. She tried to keep the surprise out of her voice, but failed miserably.

He chuckled. "The last time I checked, I haven't been banned from the hotel."

"I'm just surprised to see you here. It's been a while."

His eyes traveled around the store. "Well, things have certainly changed, Livi. You've done a nice job with this shop."

"Thank you."

"What prompted your return to Los Angeles?"

"My job mostly," she responded.

"I thought the reason you moved to San Francisco was so that you could be closer to your family."

"What's going on? Why all the questions, Harold? When did you become so interested in my life?"

"I'm just curious. That's all."

"How have you been?" she asked.

Harold grinned. "I'm fine. I couldn't be better."

Livi lowered her voice to a whisper. "Why are you really here, Harold? I know you didn't come here just to see me."

"I'm having lunch with my sister and since I was here, I thought I'd come say hello."

Livi folded her arms across her chest. "Huh…that's interesting, since you never bothered to say goodbye. I called you a couple of times after I moved to San Francisco, but you never once returned my calls."

"There was a lot going on at the time."

"I'm sure."

"So, what do you think of your new employer?" Harold inquired.

"Malcolm Alexander is great. He's been very fair and generous to everyone. He reminds me a lot of Robert."

"So I've heard," Harold muttered. "You've become a part of their family, I see."

She stiffened. "Excuse me?"

"Everyone here is one big, happy family—at least that's what my sister tells me."

"Yes, I guess you can say we are," Livi responded.

"A beautiful woman like yourself—I am surprised you haven't caught the eye of one of the Alexander men."

Livi did not respond.

"Tell me something," Harold began. "Why didn't you warn me of what was about to happen? I thought that we were friends, Livi."

"Harold, I didn't know anything," she responded. "I was in transition to San Francisco. I was just as surprised as everybody else to find out that Robert had a son. He never shared that part of his life with me."

"You were his assistant."

"Right," Livi responded. "His *assistant.* You were his nephew and he never once said anything to you, either. Like anyone else, Robert had his secrets and they were his alone."

Harold scanned her face. "You had no idea that my uncle was about to screw me over? He never said a word to you?"

Livi met his gaze. "Not one word."

"The thing that gets me is that none of you sided with me. You all just left me hanging."

"Harold, there wasn't a side to choose. Robert made his decision. He didn't ask for our thoughts or opinions because they didn't matter. Robert had a legal right to leave his estate to anyone he chose."

"My uncle could have been honest with me and the rest of the family. He took the coward's way out."

"How long are you going to hold on to your anger, Harold?"

"I did everything I could to prove myself to my uncle. I just thought he..." His voice died.

"Your uncle loved you, Harold. He loved you like a son, but Robert wanted to leave his legacy to his flesh-and-blood child. Would you have done any different if you were in his shoes?"

Livi was glad to be home. She removed her shoes as soon as she entered the three-bedroom condo. She took off her jacket next.

Blaze was coming over within the hour, but she needed a few minutes to relax.

Harold's visit earlier had bothered her. She felt as if he knew something, but was waiting for her to confess.

She debated whether to mention Harold's visit to Blaze. Livi was sure that he had been on a fishing expedition for information, but she didn't know what he was looking for. Maybe it was best not to worry Blaze, since she had no proof of anything concrete.

As much as she tried, Livi could not escape the uneasy feeling that had come over her during Harold's visit. She liked him as a person, but she was not sure that she could trust him. Although he truly loved his uncle, Harold had done some underhanded things behind Robert's back, or so Robert had thought.

Most of the employees had been loyal to Robert. They frequently told him about Harold's doings, which was why Robert may have decided to leave everything to Malcolm. Perhaps he felt that his nephew did not deserve it or would not honor his final wishes.

Livi changed into a maxi sundress and fluffed up her short curls with her fingers while she waited for Blaze to arrive. She was looking forward to spending the evening with him. Livi had even pulled out a deck of cards.

She and her friends had met Blaze and his buddies the very first night in Las Vegas. They spent some time in the casino but ended up playing Spades in Livi's hotel room.

We had so much fun that night. I can't remember laughing so much.

Livi wanted to recapture those moments. If she could remind Blaze of how happy they were in Vegas, just maybe…

She let the thought linger.

I can't keep my mind off Livi.

The thought reverberated in Blaze's head several times throughout the day. He had spent the last half hour of work in a conference room with the marketing team going over the new campaign. Blaze was itching to escape because he was so distracted.

That's when he decided to call Livi. He gladly accepted her invitation to come over.

He shifted in his seat as he struggled to pay attention to the drivers on the packed freeway.

The meeting ended shortly after 5:00 p.m. and Blaze had practically run out of the room. He had originally intended to lock himself in his office in hopes of tackling the mountain of paperwork on his desk, but he was too distracted by Livi.

Blaze could not ignore the tingling in the pit of his stomach. His feelings for Livi were still present, although he fought to keep them from intensifying.

"This is crazy," he muttered. "I can't have these kinds of feelings for Livi. It's too soon."

Blaze swallowed hard. The intense attraction they felt toward each other while in Las Vegas had never dissipated. He was going to have to be careful around Livi. He wasn't ready to settle down and did not want to make her think otherwise. He enjoyed being single. With his job, Blaze wanted the freedom to come and go as he pleased.

Livi opened the front door almost as soon as he arrived. She smiled and stepped aside to let him enter.

"Have you eaten?" she asked.

Blaze shook his head no. "Would you like to go out and get something to eat?"

"I cooked dinner."

He broke into a grin. "You cook?"

She gave him a light punch on the arm. "Of course, I cook. I'll have you know that I happen to be a great cook."

"I'll be the judge of that, if you don't mind," Blaze told her.

"Dinner's ready, so why don't we eat first," Livi suggested.

Blaze sampled the shrimp scampi over linguine and asked, "You know this is my favorite, don't you?"

Livi stared with longing at him. "I remember."

"It's delicious."

She wiped her mouth on the edge of her napkin. "Thank you."

"Did I see a deck of cards on your coffee table?"

Livi broke into a short laugh. "You sure did."

"We had dinner together, went to the casino and then went back to the hotel and played Spades with our friends. We made a great team in Vegas, didn't we?"

Livi nodded. "I thought so."

Their eyes met and held.

She broke the gaze and tried to stem the dizzying current racing through her. "I have a confession to make."

"What is it?" Blaze asked. He took a long sip of his iced tea.

"I did not make dessert," Livi stated. "I would have, but I didn't have enough time."

He laughed.

"You have a wonderful laugh, Blaze. I love listening to it."

"I admire your zest for living."

"I believe in living life to the fullest—this way you have no regrets as your life comes to an end."

Blaze wiped his mouth, and then asked, "So you have no regrets?"

"One," she answered but did not elaborate.

After dinner, they settled down in the living room, and kept the conversation light.

Livi picked up the cards. "Do you remember how badly I beat you in Spades?"

"You beat me?" Blaze shook his head. "I don't think so. I have no memory of anything like that."

"Well, why don't we play a quick game right now?" she suggested.

Blaze broke into a wide grin. "I don't think you want to do that, Livi."

She shuffled the deck of cards and placed them face-down on the table.

Livi sank down to the floor.

Blaze followed suit.

He drew the first card. "I have a ten."

Livi drew next. "You go first. I have a four."

She laughed at the expression on his face when he drew the next card. "What's wrong?"

"I'm fine. I got this."

Livi won the first round.

"Okay. Okay," Blaze said. "I'll give you that round."

"You're not giving me anything," she responded with a laugh. "I won that round fair and square."

"I'd forgotten how competitive you are." Blaze hadn't had this much fun in a long time. He felt an eager affection coming from Livi. Every time her gaze met his, Blaze's heart turned over in response.

"It's your turn," Livi said, bringing him out of his reverie.

Blaze won the second round. "Okay, we are going to have to play one more game to decide the winner."

Livi nodded in agreement.

It was hard to keep his attention on the game. Blaze's gaze raked boldly over Livi, dropping from her eyes to her shoulders to the creamy expanse of her neck. He was physically attracted to Livi, but he was just as attracted to her mind. She possessed a strong spirit, which he admired.

"Playing Spades with you in Vegas," Blaze murmured, "is one of my favorite memories, but what I remember most vividly is your smile and the way you looked at me. Livi, I want to be the man I see reflected in your eyes."

"You are that man," she responded softly.

His heart jolted and his pulse pounded. Livi had stoked a gently growing fire.

"I guess we need to get back to our game."

Livi nodded.

"I guess you're the winner," he said a short time later.

Blaze checked his watch, and then said, "I should probably leave. I have a lot of work on my desk waiting for me bright and early in the morning."

He rose to his feet and then helped Livi up.

They stood facing one another.

Blaze embraced her and planted a gentle kiss on her lips. "If you have no plans for the weekend, let's get together."

"Give me a call," she responded.

He hesitated a moment before walking to the door. When he reached the knob, he turned around to face Livi.

"Blaze…"

He tingled as she said his name. Livi's nearness kindled feelings of fire. Blaze would have preferred to sweep her into his arms and hold her close to him for a long time. He wanted to capture her full lips with his own, kissing her passionately.

"I'd better go," he whispered.

"Good night," she responded with a soft smile.

Blaze forced all thoughts of making love to Livi out of his mind, especially since he was on his way home to an empty condo. The first thing he intended to do was jump into a cold shower. He needed to cool his desires.

Livi had found her way into his heart and he hungered to be near her.

If he were hoping to keep from falling in love with Livi, Blaze was already in trouble.

Chapter 10

Livi stood in the back of the conference room where Ari Alexander had summoned everyone for a company-wide meeting. She eyed the numerous women in the audience. Even in a crowd, Blaze's presence was compelling. Some of the ladies were flipping their hair, and eyeing Blaze seductively. Before the meeting started, several women approached Blaze, grinning and batting their eyelashes.

Livi found their actions disdainful.

I can't believe the gall of these women, she thought smugly. *I never acted so cheaply. I was never so obvious.*

Her gaze strayed back to Blaze. Livi allowed her eyes to linger, appreciating the strong lines of his well-formed cheek and jaw, but it was those gray eyes of his that arrested her—intelligent eyes that seemed to peer through to her very soul.

She studied him with the sensitivity of an artist, taking in his arched brows, the faint lines above his forehead and the full upturned edges. He was wearing expensive silk trousers in an olive color, a cream-colored, long-sleeved shirt and Italian loafers.

"He's so handsome, isn't he?"

Livi glanced over at the woman standing beside her. "Excuse me?"

"I was talking about Blaze Alexander. He is *so* handsome. Ari is, too, but he has a wife."

She wanted to say, *Blaze has me.*

"I heard he's been coming by the boutique lately."

Livi turned to face the young woman. "Who told you that?"

"A couple of people. Every time Blaze comes into the hotel, we know about it."

"I'm not sure he would appreciate the employees keeping tabs on him like that," Livi stated.

"It's not as if anyone is going to tell him," the woman responded. "He's single and he's fine. There's nothing wrong with us looking."

Livi shrugged nonchalantly, and then walked over to an empty chair ten rows from the front. She stole a peek at Blaze and found him watching her. Livi gave him a tiny smile before dropping her eyes.

She chuckled softly as the woman she had been talking to rushed forward and practically leapt over a chair to sit down in the second row.

Ari stood at the podium and greeted everyone.

Like the other women in the room, it was hard for Livi to keep her eyes off Blaze. She kept telling herself that she had every right to devour him with her gaze, whether he wanted to acknowledge it or not.

It was Blaze's turn to discuss the company's marketing plans, and what those plans meant for the employees.

Livi hung on his every word, just as every other single woman in the room did.

Blaze's eyes bounced around the room, and then settled on her briefly. There was a hint of a secret smile that made Livi's heart leap.

It warmed Livi to the core because that tiny smile was reserved only for her. It felt as if they were becoming close, but she did not want to assume too much.

Livi had to find the right time to tell him more about their time in Vegas. Deep down, she prayed he would realize that they belonged together.

The evening of the charity gala arrived.

Livi stood in front of her full-length mirror, eyeing her gown. It featured a ruched bodice and a sweetheart neckline with crystal and pearl beading. The layers and ruffles of organza created a soft flowing skirt that flattered her curves.

She wore her hair slicked back with a side part.

Livi walked over to her jewelry box to search for the perfect earrings. She located the pair she was looking for and returned to the mirror to survey her reflection.

"Nooo..." She felt like crying when one of the earrings broke as she was trying to put it on. "This can't be happening."

Blaze was prompt, as usual.

He openly admired Livi as she stood in the center of her living room. "You look stunning," he told her.

His eyes traveled from her head to her feet, looking her over seductively.

She warmed beneath his gaze. It had been some time since any man had looked at her in that way.

"Mr. Alexander, I must say that you look handsome tonight. You wear a tuxedo very well."

He broke into a grin. "Why thank you, ma'am."

She pointed to her ear. "I just broke my earring so I need to see if I can find another pair."

"Wait," Blaze said. "I wanted to get you something special for tonight." He pulled out a small black velvet box.

Her brows rose in surprise. "What's this?"

"Look inside and see."

Livi peered into the box and broke into a wide grin. "Blaze Alexander, you are my hero. These earrings are perfect."

The delicate pearl-and-diamond earrings were the ideal accessory for her gown. They even matched her necklace.

Livi moved toward him, impelled involuntarily by her own desire, and kissed him.

The kiss sent the pit of her stomach into a wild swirl.

Livi stepped away from him. "Thank you."

Blaze watched as she put them on, and then nodded his approval. "When I saw them in the store, I knew they were you."

Ten minutes later, they took the elevator down to the lobby, and strolled hand in hand through the exit doors.

Blaze led Livi to the waiting limo.

"Did you see the look that woman just gave you?" she asked when they were seated inside.

"What woman?"

"The one who was in the lobby when we came down," Livi responded. "She looked as if she wanted to eat you alive."

Blaze threw back his head and laughed.

"You do know that you have that effect on women, don't you?"

He glanced at her. "What effect?"

"Women find you irresistible, Blaze. Hey, you're charming, sexy, but there's not a hint of arrogance about you."

"I'm just being me."

"That's what's so great about you. You're a very humble man and that quality makes you even more attractive."

Blaze gave her a tiny smile. "I don't want to talk about me. Let's focus on you tonight."

Livi shook her head as she laughed. "Oh, no. We're getting reacquainted. I want to know just as much about you as you want to know about me."

Blaze escorted her to the ballroom where the charity event was being held.

On this night, celebrities headlined the fiftieth anniversary celebration of the St. Mark Children's Research Hospital, held at the Beverly Hills Hotel. The star-studded benefit gala was also commemorating what would have been the founder's one hundredth birthday. Blaze and his family were ardent supporters of St. Mark and had been for years.

"I didn't know your family would be here," Livi whispered.

"C'mon," Blaze said as if sensing her hesitation. "It's not as if you're a stranger. You've already met my parents and Ari. I'm sure you probably know Sage, too. She practically lives in the boutique."

Livi grinned. "What are you trying to say about your sister?"

"She loves to shop."

"I love shopping, too," Livi whispered.

"It's an observation, not a complaint," Blaze said with a smile.

They walked over to the table that had been reserved for the Alexander family.

"Everyone, this is Livi," Blaze announced.

Barbara embraced her. "Livi, it's nice to see you. I'm glad you could join us."

"It's very nice to finally meet you," she responded.

"I've heard some wonderful things about you and what you've done with the boutique. I stopped by there to say hello…I guess it was shortly after you started, but you were out."

Malcolm acknowledged her by shaking her hand. "You're the little lady who keeps us in business by finding all those pretty items in the boutique. You have exquisite taste."

"She does," Sage interjected. "I love the shoes and purse collections."

Blaze gave Livi a knowing grin.

Sage introduced Livi to her husband, Ryan.

Just as Blaze pulled out a chair for Livi to sit down, Ari and his wife, Natasha, joined them, followed by Drayden and his date.

Natasha sat on the right side of Livi. "I love your gown," she said. "Was this at the boutique?"

Livi nodded. "I grabbed it as soon as it came in last week."

Blaze was seated on Livi's left. "That's right. You two worked together when Livi worked for Robert."

Natasha nodded. "We did briefly. I left to start my own company shortly after Livi came on board, but we became good friends."

They halted their conversation and turned their attention to the mayor's wife, one of the co-chairs of the gala, who walked across the stage and stood at the podium. Livi's gaze slowly traveled the room, taking in all the celebrities and VIPs in attendance. She was here with Blaze Alexander. Livi felt like pinching herself just to make sure she was not dreaming.

"You look deep in thought," Blaze commented.

"I can't believe that I'm actually here with you. I know it sounds silly, but it's true. Blaze, I really appreciate your bringing me here tonight," Livi told him. "This is such a worthy cause and to be in this room with these people—people who care so much about children—I'm just thrilled to be a part of it."

"I see I'm not the only one who loves children."

"Guilty as charged," Livi responded with a smile.

Blaze and Ari excused themselves to go get drinks.

Natasha leaned over and whispered, "Look at you, Livi. You have got to tell me how you and Blaze got together."

"It was pretty simple," Livi responded. "He came into the boutique with Joshua to pick out your birthday present. We started talking and…well, here we are."

"I hope it develops into something more," Natasha said. "You two look good together."

Livi gave Natasha a tiny smile.

* * *

Upon entering the ballroom, Blaze felt as if he and Livi were under the microscope as members of the media scoured the crowd in search of the Hollywood elite and other VIPs attending the charity benefit.

Blaze focused his attention on Livi, who seemed to be thoroughly enjoying herself. He silently observed how she interacted with his family. She seemed nervous when they first arrived, but her discomfort had quickly dissipated. He knew that his family would receive her warmly.

They dined on breast of chicken Mediterranean served with sautéed artichokes, goat cheese mashed potatoes and herbed Italian vegetables. For dessert, there was mascarpone caramel cake, which Livi turned down.

"I'm stuffed," she whispered to Blaze.

Blaze agreed as he wiped his mouth with the edge of his napkin.

He smiled politely when someone snapped a picture of him, and then said, "At least they could let me eat in peace."

Sage chuckled. "I still can't believe how shy you are when it comes to stuff like this."

Blaze gave her a narrowed glance. "You know how I feel about being in the public eye, sis. I can't stand it."

"You're the vice president of sales and marketing for the Alexander-DePaul Group, Blaze," she responded, raising fine, arched eyebrows. "You'd better get used to this because it's not going to go away."

"Why do you hate it so much?" Livi asked. "All the attention."

"I just value my privacy."

"Have you always been this way?"

"Yes," he responded.

"I'm the same way," Livi told him. "I would rather live outside the limelight."

Blaze decided he was not going to let a little media attention ruin his night with Livi. He placed his hand on top of hers and rubbed it gently.

Livi looked up and met Barbara's gaze. Blaze's mom winked and smiled in approval.

At the end of the evening, Blaze escorted Livi out of the hotel. Members of his family walked out with them.

Blaze took Livi up to her condo.

"Thank you for tonight," Livi said. "I had a wonderful time."

"Almost feels like old times, huh?"

She nodded. "I still can't believe that we've been able to reconnect after all this time. It doesn't feel like there's a two-year gap between the last time we saw each other."

"It could have been much sooner, Livi."

"I know," she murmured. "You're never going to let me live that down, are you?"

"We wasted almost two years of our lives. Who knows what could have happened if we'd stayed in contact?"

"Blaze, I just didn't know how to approach you. I knew that the day would come when we would come face-to-face, but...I guess I let time slip away."

It was too easy to get lost in the way Livi looked at him. Blaze's heart lurched madly. He cleared his throat, pretending not to be affected.

"I'm glad I found you," he said in a low voice. "At least now I can see where this is going. I don't have to wonder about what could have been."

"What are you saying, Blaze?" Livi asked.

"Isn't it obvious? I have feelings for you and I'd like to explore those feelings." He took her face in his hand and held it gently.

"You have haunted my dreams since the moment we met in Vegas," Blaze told her. He touched his lips to hers, and then gently covered her mouth.

The caress of his lips on Livi's mouth set her aflame. His moist, firm mouth demanded a response.

She kissed him back.

"Your lips are as sweet as I remembered."

Livi smiled. "It's about time you gave me a real kiss."

His eyebrows rose in surprise. "I didn't want to rush you into anything."

She nodded. "I understand and I appreciate that, but—"

His lips recaptured hers, more demanding this time. Sparks of desire ignited in the pit of his stomach.

Although he did not want to leave, Blaze decided that it was best to do so. He kissed her once more before saying, "It's late. I should be heading home." Blaze's desire for Livi was still as strong as ever; even now, he fantasized about ripping the gorgeous gown off that sexy body of hers.

Livi nodded. "I can hear Sybil moving around in her room. I'm sure she's waiting for you to leave so that she can grill me about our date."

Although Blaze knew that both he and Livi wanted to make love, it would only complicate and confuse their growing relationship. He turned to leave.

Livi lingered in the doorway as she watched Blaze walk toward the elevator. More than anything, she wanted to call out to him to come back and never leave her side. She was more certain than ever that she wanted Blaze Alexander all to herself.

Chapter 11

From everything Livi had read about Blaze, she knew he was a confirmed bachelor. Although he was still attracted to her, he might not be interested.

Livi was experiencing mixed emotions when it came to Blaze. She now wished for a chance to relive their special time in Vegas. She would not run away, but stay and try to sort out the situation in a mature manner. Sadly, there were no do-overs in life.

Livi got up and made her way to the master bedroom. Inside, she removed her gown and padded barefoot into the bathroom. Livi showered quickly. She slipped on a silky nightgown with a matching robe.

Ten minutes later, there was a soft knock on her bedroom door.

"What took you so long?" she asked with a grin.

"So how did it go tonight?" Sybil wanted to know.

"It was great," Livi responded. "We had a good time together. His parents were there and they're both really nice people."

"I noticed that he was here for a while. I figured I'd be seeing you in the morning."

"It's too soon for a physical relationship," Livi explained. "We're taking things slow."

They settled down on her bed to continue their conversation.

"He's absolutely gorgeous," Livi stated. "You should have seen him in his tux earlier. I had a hard time keeping my eyes off him. Everything I felt tonight… It was like we haven't spent one day apart."

"Sounds to me like you two are meant to be, Livi."

"I think so, too. But I'm not sure Blaze is looking for a serious relationship."

"Did he tell you that?"

Livi shook her head no. "Not in so many words. Blaze did say that he wanted to explore where this one is heading, but I'm not exactly sure what that means."

"If you want Blaze, then you're going to have to go after him, Livi," Sybil advised. "If I were you, I wouldn't let him just walk out of my life. I'm just saying…"

Livi contemplated her friend's words.

"You do want him, don't you?" Sybil asked.

She nodded. "I do. I want Blaze in my life. He's a good man and I'm crazy about him."

"Then go get your man."

Livi's skin prickled with excitement. She was going to do just as Sybil suggested. She was going to win Blaze's heart.

* * *

It was a constant battle for Blaze to keep his mind off Livi. She had preoccupied his thoughts all night and then again the following day. He had come into the office on Saturday to get some work done, but he hadn't accomplished much because of his distraction.

The knock on his door drew his thoughts to the present.

"Sage, what are you doing here? I thought you and Ryan were flying to New York today."

"We're leaving for the airport in a few," she responded. "I came here to drop off a packet of information Daddy needs for his meeting on Monday. Ryan and I will be in New York for the next two weeks."

"Try not to shop too much."

Sage sent her brother a sharp glare. "Speaking of shopping, when did you pick up Livi Carlyle?"

Blaze chuckled. "I didn't just pick her up. I've gotten to know her pretty well and so I asked her to be my date for the gala."

"You two look good together," Sage told him. "She's a lovely person."

"Livi is very sweet," Blaze responded. "But trust me. I am okay with the way things are between us. I don't want to rush into anything serious."

"You know that she likes you."

He met his sister's gaze. "You really think so?"

Sage nodded. "And I have a suspicion that you care for Livi just as much."

"Yes, I care deeply for her," Blaze confessed. "To be honest, I never expected to have such strong feelings for Livi."

"Life is short and fleeting, Blaze," Sage reminded him. "Don't waste a moment of it."

"I'll remember that."

As soon as Sage left his office, Blaze picked up the telephone.

"Livi, how are you?"

"I'm fine," she responded. "How are you doing?"

Blaze laughed. "We sound like a couple of high school students, don't we?"

"Yeah," Livi agreed.

"You were on my mind, so I thought I'd give you a call."

"It's good to hear from you, Blaze. To be honest, I was hoping you would call me."

"Livi, you know that you could have called me. The telephone works both ways."

"I thought about it," she admitted. "I just didn't want to be pushy."

"I would never consider you to be a pushy person, Livi."

"Understood."

"Good," Blaze murmured. "Now for the reason for my call. We're giving my dad a surprise birthday party in a couple of weeks. I'd like you to be my date."

There was a slight pause, and then Livi responded, "Really?"

"Yes," Blaze said.

"I would love that."

As soon as he hung up the phone, Blaze began to have second thoughts. Maybe he should not have invited her to such an intimate family event. He hoped it would not send her the wrong message.

* * *

Livi tried on three different gowns in her boutique, but none of them shouted *perfect.*

"You must be going someplace pretty special," Martha said. "Are you going with Blaze Alexander?"

Livi nodded. "But we're just friends."

Martha's expression showed that she clearly did not believe Livi. "You're going through a lot of trouble for someone who isn't special to you."

Livi pulled another dress off the rack and frowned. "I guess I'll run down the street during lunch to see if the shop there has anything."

"That's a beautiful dress," Natasha said as she walked into the boutique. "It'll look great on you."

"You really think so?" Livi asked.

Natasha nodded. "That color is perfect for your complexion. Have you tried it on?"

"No." Lowering her voice, Livi said, "Blaze asked me to accompany him to your father-in-law's birthday party. I'm trying to find the perfect dress."

"I think you already have. I love this one."

Livi eyed the dress on the hanger. "I like it, but I don't know if it's dressy enough for a party like that." She was careful to keep her voice low because she knew Martha was trying to eavesdrop on her conversation.

"It's perfect," Natasha assured her. "It's simple but elegant."

"That's usually my style," Livi said. "I just thought I'd change it up some."

Natasha shook her head no. "I wouldn't. Wear what works for you."

"I'll try it on."

Livi eyed her reflection in the three-way mirror and

smiled. The dress actually looked much better draped on her body than on the hanger.

"You look great," Natasha and Martha said in unison.

"Natasha, I think you're right about this dress," Livi stated. "I'm loving it."

She made her decision, and then went back to the dressing room to change out of the dress.

When Livi walked out a few minutes later, Natasha met her and said, "I'm glad Blaze is bringing you to the party. I think you two make a great couple."

"We're not a couple, Natasha."

"Maybe not, but do you want to rule it out?"

Livi did not respond. Deep down, she wished she could confide in Natasha, but Livi was not about to betray Blaze.

Natasha pointed to a pair of shoes. "When I was in Sacramento a couple of weeks ago, I saw those pumps in a burgundy color. Do you have them in stock?"

"We don't," Livi responded, "but I can special-order them for you. They also come in an olive green that would match the suit you're wearing."

Natasha's eyes lit up. "Order a pair in olive for me, as well. Size 8."

Livi finalized Natasha's order. "They'll arrive in seven to ten days."

"I can't wait."

They talked for a few minutes more, and then Natasha left the boutique and walked in the direction of the exit doors leading to the parking garage.

She felt a thread of guilt over the secret she was keeping. Livi liked and respected Natasha. She hoped her friend would be able to forgive her one day.

Chapter 12

Blaze and Livi arrived at the marina and quickly boarded the yacht. His parents were due to arrive within the hour.

Everyone was already on board except for Kellen and his date.

"Where is that boy?" Sage questioned. "He was supposed to be here by now."

Zaire chuckled. "Probably getting busy with that new girlfriend of his."

"Surely that could have waited until after the party," Sage responded stiffly, prompting laughter from Blaze and Livi.

"Here they are," Ryan announced. "Relax, sweetheart. I don't want you getting upset. It's not good for the baby."

Sage lit into her brother as soon as he stepped on

board. "You know this is supposed to be a surprise party," she fussed.

"I'm here already," Kellen responded. "Calm down, sis. Let's just enjoy the evening."

Several of Malcolm's close friends arrived and joined the family in the lounge area, which included a full bar, cigar deck and dance floor. The second-story lounge was complete with several overstuffed sofas, romantic lanterns and tropical plants.

Livi admired the Polynesian-style décor that was both modern and elegant. Blaze took her from room to room, giving her a tour of the luxury yacht. "This is just beautiful," she said.

"My mom fell in love with this yacht the moment she saw it, so she bought it as a gift for my dad."

"It's a very nice gift."

Blaze agreed. "Dad always dreamed of buying one, but this is not something he would buy for himself. My parents know each other well. I think that's one of the reasons their marriage works. That and the fact that they are still head over heels in love."

Livi smiled. "My parents have a good marriage, too, but for them it's not about the passion. They are both astute businesspeople and they seem to run their marriage in the same way that they run their company." She shrugged. "It works for them."

"My mother says that it's important to be able to anticipate the desires of your spouse and put their needs before your own."

Livi nodded. "I agree with her."

As they awaited the arrival of the guest of honor, attendees were given a glass of champagne.

"This is really nice," Livi said. "You have a steel-drum band and hula dancers?"

He nodded. "We also have a DJ."

"Wow, you all did a wonderful job putting this together."

"I can't take credit for any of this. Sage, Ari and Natasha handled all the arrangements."

Blaze took Livi to the upper deck where an array of appetizers was spread out for guests.

At one end of the table there was a tropical fruit-and-cheese display with assorted crackers, mini-crab cakes and spinach-artichoke dip. The other end offered a brie and raspberry cream cheese display, salsa and a hot tuna dip. In the middle were teriyaki chicken strips with ponzu dip, and jumbo shrimp with a spicy cocktail sauce.

"Everything looks delicious. I'm tempted to try everything, but then I'd have to spend the rest of the weekend on a treadmill." Livi felt the heat of Blaze's gaze on her and looked up. "Why are you staring at me like that?"

"Was I staring? I'm sorry."

"The limo is pulling into the marina," Zaire announced. "We need to go inside to the lounge."

Blaze took Livi by the hand and led her down to the second level.

His touch warmed her all over. Livi savored the feel of his skin and the scent of his cologne, which was almost intoxicating.

Why did I ever run away from this man? she wondered.

They stood in silence, waiting for Malcolm and Barbara to enter the lounge.

"Why is it so dark in here?" she heard him say before the lights came on and everyone yelled, "SURPRISE!"

Malcolm looked down at his grinning wife and picked her up. He kissed her before releasing her. "I know you're behind this."

"Happy birthday, sugar," she murmured, her gaze never leaving Malcolm's face. It was clear that Barbara only had eyes for her husband.

Blaze and his siblings joined their parents.

Livi watched them, a smile on her face. She and her parents were close, and she liked that Blaze also came from a close-knit family. Livi did not have any siblings, however, and she envied him in that respect.

Now that Malcolm and Barbara had arrived, everyone went into the dining area where a pasta station was set up with choices of salmon alfredo, shrimp scampi and meatball marinara. A carving station of top sirloin was also set up on the opposite side of the room.

While the guests ate, the hula dancers performed to the rhythm of the steel-drum band.

"If I weren't pregnant, I could do that," Sage stated.

Livi's eyes widened in surprise. "You're going to have a baby, too?" She knew that Natasha was pregnant, but she hadn't known about Sage.

"Yes. Ryan and I can't wait to meet this little person."

Livi felt a twinge of sadness. For a brief moment, she allowed herself to fantasize about having a "little" Blaze. She flushed at the thought of being pregnant with his child. The thought was premature, but she couldn't just dismiss the idea out of hand. Livi wanted to have children with Blaze one day. She knew that he would be a great father.

"Would you like to dance?" Blaze asked Livi after they had eaten.

She nodded. "I love dancing—don't you remember? I just haven't done it in a long time."

He eyed her in amazement. "What? Not the party animal herself..."

"Ha-ha," she muttered, taking him by the hand. "I hope you learned something other than that two-step you used to do."

Blaze pretended to be offended. "I know you're not talking about me. Girl, you must be thinking about some other guy."

Livi laughed as she rose to her feet, waiting for Blaze to take her to the dance floor. Sage and Ryan were on their heels.

She walked slowly, her body swaying to the music. "I love this song."

Blaze escorted her to the middle of the front of the dance floor and began dancing to the music.

"Yeah," Livi uttered with a laugh. "You're still doing that two-step move."

Blaze changed it up, surprising her.

"Wow, look at you."

"I have some moves," he bragged. "I didn't show you everything."

One song ended and a slow one began while they were still on the dance floor.

Blaze's hands locked against her spine.

Livi relaxed, sinking into his cushioning embrace. Her skin tingled from the contact. She met his gaze.

"There's so much I want to say to you," she blurted out.

He smiled. "I feel the same way."

The song ended, but Blaze did not release Livi.

Kellen walked over and tapped Blaze on the shoulder. "Can I dance with the pretty lady?"

His date sashayed toward them. "I'll take Blaze off your hands."

Afterwards, Livi and Blaze took a stroll on the deck.

Livi paused and pointed to a small boat carrying two people. "Are they taking pictures of us?"

Blaze nodded. "This is the part of my life that I'm not feeling," he told Livi.

She slipped her arm through his. "The price of fame, huh?"

He nodded. "We can't even have a private party for my father without someone trying to make it a headline in the news. It's ridiculous."

"We can go back inside if you want," Livi suggested.

Blaze shook his head no. "I'm fine."

"I need to tell you something," Livi began.

"What is it?" he asked.

They walked over to a couple of lounge chairs and sat down.

"Blaze, I have feelings for you," she confessed.

"Livi, I care for you, too."

"When we were in Vegas, a lot happened between us." Livi tried to search for the right words. "I don't quite know where to begin."

"Things were heavy and intense between us," Blaze interjected. "That's why I don't want to rush the relationship. Back then, we didn't know if we would ever see each other again. But now…I'm not going anywhere."

"Neither am I," Livi stated.

She wanted to tell him everything that happened in Vegas, but held back for now. Livi had planned to confess all as soon as they were alone. She no longer wanted to carry this secret.

A few minutes later, Blaze and Livi walked back inside and headed straight to the dance floor.

At the end of the evening, guests were given a choice of an iPad case or a notepad, pen and flash drive set by Ungaro as a party favor. Blaze gave Livi one of each.

When they were inside his car, he glanced over at Livi and asked, "Are you ready to go home?"

"What do you have in mind?"

"I thought that maybe we could go back to my place and talk."

"Finally, some privacy," Blaze uttered as he escorted Livi into his apartment. "No media lurking around. I don't have to be on guard."

"I don't think you should let them get to you like this," Livi stated. "You just have to pretend that they aren't there."

Their gazes locked and both of them could see the attraction mirrored in the other's eyes.

The smoldering flame Livi saw in his eyes startled her. She was by no means blind to his attraction, but the intensity of his gaze...Livi needed to tell him the truth.

Before she could open her mouth to speak, Blaze pulled her into his arms. "Livi, there is something that I've wanted to do all evening." The prolonged anticipation of kissing her had become unbearable. His mouth covered hers hungrily.

Raising his mouth from hers, Blaze gazed lovingly into her eyes.

Livi drew his face to hers in a renewed embrace. Her

body ached for his touch and she no longer wanted to deny herself.

He kissed her again, lingering, savoring every moment.

"There are no words to describe how badly I want to make love to you," Blaze whispered.

Livi's emotions whirled. Blood pounded in her brain, leapt from her heart and made her knees tremble.

"This is something we both want," she said huskily.

There was a pensive shimmer in the shadow of his eye.

"I want this as much as you do, Blaze."

Blaze gathered her into his arms and held her snugly. "I have really missed you."

He touched his lips to hers.

Livi kissed him with a passionate hunger that belied her outward calm. She was shocked by her own eager response.

She felt blissfully content and fully alive.

Livi wrapped her arms around Blaze, pulling him closer to her. She could feel his uneven breathing on her cheek, as he held her tightly.

Blaze traced his fingertip across her lips, causing Livi's skin to tingle when he touched her. He paused to kiss her, sending currents of desire through her.

"Make love to me," she whispered between kisses.

"You don't know how badly I've wanted to hear those words. I've wanted you from the moment I saw you again."

Blaze bent his head and captured her lips in a demanding kiss.

Locking her hands behind his neck, Livi returned his kiss, matching passion for passion.

Blaze picked her up and carried her into his bedroom. He undressed her slowly.

"You are so beautiful," he told her in a husky voice.

His mouth covered hers again, hungrily.

A fiery passion ignited in the pit of Livi's belly as she and Blaze were joined in a lover's dance. Although she did not give voice to the love she felt for Blaze, Livi tried to show him in her gaze, her kisses and the rhythm of her movement.

She focused only on this moment and Blaze, forgetting her secret for the time being. Nothing else mattered.

Blaze woke shortly after seven the next morning. A smile spread across his face as he watched Livi sleep. She still looked beautiful with her short hair spiked in every direction.

Last night had been perfect but commitment could not be based on great sex. Blaze found it very easy being with Livi. She was intelligent, very independent and sexy.

Blaze planted tiny kisses on each cheek, her nose, her chin and her neck in an attempt to wake her up.

Livi moaned softly.

He placed a kiss on her lips.

Livi opened her eyes, stretched and yawned. "Good morning."

She sat up in bed, pulling the covers up to hide her breasts.

"How did you sleep?" he asked.

Livi smiled. "You mean after you finally let me get some sleep?"

She attempted to get out of bed, but Blaze held her hostage. "Not just yet."

"I need to take a shower."

"Do you mind if I join you?"

Livi planted a kiss on his lips. "Not at all."

She got out of bed and padded barefoot across the floor into the bathroom.

Blaze could hear the shower running and climbed out of bed. Before he could join Livi, the telephone rang.

"Hello?"

Blaze's smile disappeared and he felt as if all blood had drained from his face. "Excuse me?"

"Is it true that you and Livi Carlyle are married and have been for two years?"

He slammed down the telephone.

He and Livi married? What craziness was this?

The phone rang again.

He picked up the receiver and it was another reporter.

Blaze hung up the phone.

His stomach was filled with apprehension. He couldn't understand why they were asking him about a nonexistent marriage to Livi. Reporters would go to any lengths to get a story, it seemed.

Had this news already reached his parents? Blaze did not know whether to call them or just do nothing. He did not want to upset them over what was clearly a lie.

Both his cell and home phone were ringing.

Blaze ignored the home phone and answered his cell. "Hello? Leave me alone," he yelled into the receiver.

"Who was that?" Livi inquired as she walked out of the bathroom wrapped in a large fluffy towel.

"That was a reporter," Blaze announced. "He wanted confirmation on our marriage. The phone's been ringing off the hook. Can you believe this?"

Shocked, she uttered, "He wanted *what?*"

Blaze eyed her hard. "I don't know where they got the impression that we're married, but it's a ridiculous claim." His voice was hard. "I'm going to call Ira and have him file a lawsuit. This is so—"

"Blaze…we need to talk," she quickly interjected.

He scanned her face. "Do you know something about this?"

"I…the last day in Vegas…" Livi swallowed hard. "Blaze, we got married."

His body stiffened in shock and he put a hand to his head. "No…"

Livi wrapped the towel tighter around her body. "It's true. You and I are married."

Blaze stood there shaking his head in disbelief. "That can't be true."

She walked over to her purse and pulled out several pieces of paper.

Livi handed them to Blaze. "This is our marriage license and the vows we wrote down on napkins."

"Why didn't you tell me?" he asked after a long silence.

"Blaze, I wanted a chance for us to get reacquainted before springing something like this on you."

"You're good at keeping secrets," he uttered coldly. "At least from me, anyway. Who did you sell the story to?"

"You think I did this?"

"How else could they have found out?" Blaze demanded.

"I don't know, but I had nothing to do with this. I haven't told a soul about our marriage. I had planned to tell you last night, but then…" Her voice died as her eyes filled with tears. "I didn't do this."

He sat down on the edge of the bed.

Livi sat down beside him. "I'm so sorry you had to find out this way. I was going to tell you this morning, but the media beat me to it. I want to tell you everything."

She reached for his hand, but he rose to his feet and began pacing back and forth.

Livi blinked rapidly. "What? Blaze, do you really believe I'm the one responsible for this?"

"Who else could it be?" he asked, spacing the words evenly.

The telephone rang, cutting the silence.

Blaze did not bother to answer it.

He crossed the room in quick angry strides and peeked out the window. "There's a news van outside." Blaze sighed with exasperation.

Livi stood up and followed him.

"I didn't have anything to do with this, Blaze."

He turned and looked down at her. "I don't even know who you are, Livi. You are definitely not the woman I thought you were."

"*Wow.* I can't believe you just said that to me." Livi began putting on her clothes. "I need to get out of here."

"If they see you leaving here now, it would only confirm our marriage."

"They already know that we've been seeing each other. My being here just confirms that I spent the night here." Livi slipped on her shoes. "I'm not going to sit around here and have you toss accusations my way. They are reporters and somehow they found out that we're married. I had nothing to do with it, Blaze. I'm only guilty of not telling you before you found out this way."

"My family..." Blaze said as he placed his hands to his face.

She picked up the towel and folded it. "I'm sure they will understand."

"I really thought I could trust you." His tone was coolly disapproving.

"Blaze, I didn't do this," Livi repeated once more. "I've kept our marriage a secret all this time, so why would I suddenly shout it to the world now?"

"Maybe it's because you don't want to end the marriage," Blaze stated with an edge to his voice. "You're married to an Alexander."

"Do you really think I'm that shallow?"

"I don't know," he responded with a shrug. "I will tell you this, Livi. We are going to get this marriage annulled as quickly as possible. I definitely don't want anything to do with someone I can't trust."

Chapter 13

Livi slipped out of the building through a back exit and hailed a taxi.

It wasn't until she was home in her own condo that she allowed her tears to flow. Livi had vowed not to break down in front of Blaze.

Sybil walked out of the guest bedroom. "Honey, what's wrong?"

Livi sat down on her sofa with her hands to her face. Tears blinded her eyes and choked her voice. She felt as if her heart were breaking into several little pieces.

Sybil handed her a tissue. "Did you and Blaze have a fight?"

She wiped her face. "Sybil, I need to tell you something, but you have to promise me that you won't get upset with me. I really can't take that right now."

"Of course, I won't be upset. What is it?"

"While we were in Las Vegas, you know that Blaze and I spent a lot of time together."

Sybil chuckled. "You just abandoned your girls, but we understood. What's going on?"

"There's something that I never told you. Blaze and I got married that last night there," Livi announced.

Her friend gasped loudly. "I know I didn't just hear you correctly. Did you say that you and Blaze Alexander are married?"

Livi nodded. "Yes. We really didn't have clear heads. In fact, Blaze didn't remember anything that happened, including the marriage."

"He didn't know that you two were married?"

Livi nodded. "I should have told him right away, but I just wanted him to spend time with me first."

"He wasn't the only one in the dark," Sybil uttered. "Why didn't you tell me and Amy? We are your girls."

"I was too embarrassed. How could I tell you that I married a man I knew for only three days? It was such a stupid thing to do."

"Why are you telling me this now?"

"Because now everyone is going to find out," Livi stated. "Somehow the news media got wind of it. Blaze is angry with me because he thinks I tipped them off. He wants to get the marriage annulled. He hates me."

"I can't believe that you're actually married to Blaze Alexander. *A very rich and handsome Blaze Alexander.*"

"I don't care about his money," Livi stated. "You know that money doesn't faze me at all."

"I can't believe that you kept me out of the loop on this," Sybil said. "Livi, you could have trusted me."

"Oh, nooo..." She groaned. "My parents. I need to call them."

"You might want to do it now before they hear about it on the news or in some tabloid." Sybil reached over and handed Livi the telephone. "While you're talking to your parents, I'm going to have Amy come over. She got in late last night, but she needs to get over here right now."

The telephone rang.

Sybil answered it. "No, this is not Livi Carlyle. I'm sorry, but you have the wrong number. Who am I? Sybil Sanderson and this is my number."

"Thank you," Livi told her.

"We're getting your number changed today."

Livi took the phone. "I'd better call my parents."

She walked into her bedroom for some privacy. While the conversation was not an easy one, Livi managed to make it through, but not without shedding tears.

When she walked out of her bedroom, Amy and Sybil were seated in the living room talking.

"What were you thinking?" Amy demanded. "You hardly knew the man."

She sank down on top of the leather ottoman. "Blaze is a sweetheart. He is kind, intelligent and generous. He has a wonderful sense of humor. We have a lot in common. And on top of that, I love him."

"She's a grown woman, Amy," Sybil interjected. "Livi feels bad enough."

"You have every right to be angry with me," Livi said, "but I can't change the past. What's done is done."

"I thought you and Blaze were seeing each other now."

"We were getting close until this happened. Now he doesn't want anything to do with me."

"I think you need to see an attorney," Sybil stated.

"Why?" Livi wanted to know. "We never had a real marriage. I don't want anything from Blaze."

"Do you really think it's going to be so cut-and-dried?" Amy asked. "What did your parents say?"

"They want me to come home so that we can come up with a game plan." Livi put a hand to her face. "I should have said something to Blaze earlier."

Amy nodded in agreement. "Does he know everything?"

Livi shook her head no. "I'm not sure he could have handled knowing the truth about me. He flipped out over the idea that we're married."

"It's going to come out, Livi, so you might as well come clean once and for all."

"I don't think you need to tell Blaze any of that until you know if he wants to stay in the marriage," Sybil stated.

She could get through this, Livi decided. She would do what she had been doing all of her life. She would survive.

Blaze was furious with himself. He should have known that Livi had something up her sleeve. Apparently, Livi was a master manipulator, willing to do anything to stay married. Blaze vowed from this moment forward that he would have nothing else to do with her.

The telephone rang.

Blaze unplugged it.

He was furious. Livi had run out on him and never bothered to let him know that they were married. Blaze could only imagine the mess he would have unknowingly had if he married another woman.

Blaze needed to tell his parents what was going on before they heard it from someone else.

He picked up his cell phone and called his father.

"Dad, we need to have an emergency meeting," Blaze announced when Malcolm answered. "The whole family."

"What's going on, Blaze?"

Blaze heard the concern in his father's voice and felt bad.

"This is not something that should be discussed over the telephone. I'll tell you when I get there."

They ended the call.

His cell rang and it was his father.

"Everyone will be here within the hour." After a brief pause, he said, "I just received a phone call from a reporter."

"I figured you might. Dad…"

"We'll finish the conversation when you get here."

Blaze could hear the disappointment in his father's voice. Waves of guilt flowed through him. He had hoped to never hurt them again.

He could not believe that he and Livi were married. So that night when he got on stage with his frat brothers…they had eloped earlier in the day. His frat brothers never said anything, so he assumed he hadn't told them. Maybe he and Livi were waiting to share their news until after the concert.

His fall changed everything, but it made no sense that Livi had run off. They had attended the concert together.

Blaze shrugged. It no longer mattered. The only thing on his mind was annulling the marriage. It had clearly been a mistake.

If he ever saw Livi again, it would be much too soon.

* * *

Livi debated whether to go into the boutique, but she had a sale to prepare for. Besides, she needed to stay busy to keep her mind off Blaze.

A woman entered the store and Livi greeted her.

She noted the way the woman kept watching her when she thought Livi wasn't aware of it. Her gaze traveled to Martha, who had a look of suspicion in her expression.

Martha picked up the phone and made a quick phone call.

The woman approached Livi. "Can you please confirm that you're married to Blaze Alexander? Why did you keep your marriage a secret?"

Security rushed in and quickly escorted her out.

Seconds later, Natasha blew into the boutique and asked, "Are you okay?"

Livi nodded. "I guess you've heard what the media is saying."

She gave a sympathetic nod. "We're all heading to Pacific Palisades to discuss how to move forward." She glanced around the boutique before adding, "I think you should come with us."

Livi shook her head no. "I don't think so. Blaze is furious with me. He thinks that I'm the one who alerted the media."

"Are you and Blaze married?" Natasha asked in a whisper.

She nodded.

"I think that you need to see this." Natasha handed her a newspaper. "It was delivered to us this morning."

Splashed across the front was a photo of her and Blaze. "Oh, nooo…" Livi groaned.

"They are claiming to have a copy of the marriage license."

"I didn't do this, Natasha," Livi told her. "I never would've betrayed Blaze like this."

"I believe you." Natasha nodded in understanding.

They were joined by Ari, who said, "We need to get going."

Livi did not make a move to leave.

He glanced at her. "My parents would like for you to join us, as well. This does concern you, Livi."

To Livi, it sounded more like an order than a request.

She turned to her employee. "I'll be back shortly." Livi knew she needed to have some sort of explanation prepared for her staff upon her return. For now, she had to endure their gasps of shock and astonishment. "When I get back, I'll explain everything."

She was nervous about this meeting. No doubt Blaze had convinced all of them that she was the culprit and they would believe him. Livi worried that she might lose her job as a result of this mess.

No one said anything much during the drive to the Alexanders' oceanfront estate in Pacific Palisades. Livi was glad to have the time to gather her thoughts. The thought of having to face all of them was daunting.

Livi had been to the former DePaul estate to visit Robert or to work from the office in his exquisite Tuscan home in the Palisades Riviera community. Under normal circumstances, she would be looking forward to the visit, but not this time.

The massive home suddenly seemed intimidating. She tensed up as they pulled into the driveway of the Alexander home.

Livi hesitated. *I can call for a taxi. I don't have to go inside.*

Ari parked the car and got out.

He opened Livi's and Natasha's doors.

"It's going to be all right," Natasha whispered in a low voice. "This is not some sort of ambush. I promise."

"It feels like one," Livi mumbled.

She saw Blaze's car and her heart began to ache all over again. Her emotions were still too raw to deal with him right now. She did not know what to expect, but Livi decided that she would leave on foot, if necessary.

Chapter 14

His parents had not said much to him since his arrival, which only made Blaze feel worse. He knew they were waiting for the rest of the family to arrive, but the tense silence surrounding them was unnerving.

"What is she doing here?" Blaze demanded when Livi walked in behind Ari and Natasha. She was the last person he wanted to see.

"She's your wife," Ari stated in a tone that brooked no argument. "She should be here. This is as much about Livi as it is about you. It's time to do away with the secrets."

Before Blaze could utter a response, his parents walked out into the foyer, followed by Kellen and Zaire.

Barbara embraced Livi and said, "Welcome to the family, dear."

"Thank you," she responded softly. Livi could feel

Blaze's heated gaze on her, but she refused to look in his direction.

Malcolm embraced her next. "I echo my wife's sentiments. However, I can't wait to hear the reason behind all the secrecy. You and my son owe us an explanation. I hope it's a good one."

Sage and Ryan arrived next, a few minutes before Drayden.

With everyone present, Livi followed Blaze's parents into the family room where she took a seat on the sofa. Blaze was about to sit down in a leather wingchair, but his mother gestured toward Livi and said, "Why don't you take a seat beside your wife?"

"Mom, it's not what you think," Blaze uttered.

Barbara looked over at her husband, then back at her son. "What do you mean by that? You and Livi *are* married, right?"

Blaze nodded. "I was in Las Vegas with my frat brothers partying and just having a good time. I met Livi at that time." He paused a moment before adding, "We have been married for almost two years. However, I'm just finding out that I have a wife."

His mother could not hide her surprise. "I see, but why didn't you tell us?"

Livi stared down at her hands.

"Two years," Malcolm said. "Blaze, what were you thinking?"

"Dad, you don't understand. I had absolutely no idea about the wedding. This is a huge shock to me, as well."

"Then make me understand," his father responded. "What happened?"

"I don't know. That night, we attended a concert. My frat brothers and I were invited onto the stage to step.

I fell and suffered a head injury that caused memory loss. The doctor called it retrograde amnesia."

Barbara gasped. "Why didn't you tell us about this, son? An injury like that is serious."

Everyone looked in Livi's direction.

Livi cleared her throat noisily. "Blaze doesn't remember anything about our wedding. We were going to tell everyone after the concert, but he fell and was rushed to the hospital. The hall was so crowded—by the time I made it up to the stage, Blaze was already en route to the hospital. When I got there, I heard Blaze talking to his friends. One of them said something about his running off with me and Blaze denied it. He said that he cared for me, but that marriage was out of the question."

She gazed at Blaze for a moment before continuing. "I didn't find out that he had retrograde amnesia until we reconnected. I assumed that night that he didn't want to be married to me, so I left the hospital and went back to the hotel. My friends and I left Las Vegas the next day."

"How do you suppose news of your marriage got out?" Barbara asked.

"I have no idea," Livi answered. "I never told anyone except my parents, and I know they didn't do this."

"So why didn't you come forward then?" Malcolm wanted to know. "If the marriage was a mistake, then why not do something about it?"

"I didn't want to rush into another life-altering decision."

"So you were just going to continue this farce of a marriage?" Barbara wanted to know. "Was it in case you conceived a child?"

"In part," she responded. "I would rather be married to the father of my child, even though we were not physically together."

Blaze gave Livi a hard look.

"There is no child," she spoke directly to Blaze. "I would never keep your child from you."

He turned his attention back to his parents. "Mom, we are getting the marriage annulled as soon as possible."

"Livi, how do you feel about that?" Malcolm inquired, his arms folded across his chest. "Do you want to get your marriage annulled? I'm asking you this because I'm not buying the reason you stated. I believe there is more to this than you've said."

She stole a peek at Blaze before saying, "I've told you all the truth. We rushed into the marriage and…I just want to think this out."

"What is there to think about?" Blaze demanded.

"Don't you dare talk to me in that tone," Livi snapped. "I've had about enough of you and your attitude, Blaze Alexander. I told you that I had nothing to do with the media finding out about our marriage and that's the truth."

Ari chuckled. "You married a woman with some fire in her."

Blaze sent him a sharp glare.

The telephone rang.

"I suppose the phone will be ringing off the hook all day," Barbara murmured.

"We'll turn them off or we can get the number changed," Malcolm responded. "We are going to issue a statement and then be done with it."

"Issue a statement saying what exactly?" Blaze asked.

"We can't deny that you're married, can we?" his father responded.

Blaze's mouth tightened. "Why confirm or deny anything? My personal life is my business."

"So you would prefer that we say nothing?" his father asked.

"I don't owe the media or the world any explanations."

"This is only going to increase the curiosity about the two of you and why you've kept your marriage a secret," Barbara stated. "You're going to be hounded by the media. If you just confirm the marriage, then maybe the interest will die down."

Ari and Malcolm nodded in agreement.

Blaze looked at Natasha. "What do you think? Do you agree with them?"

"You are entitled to your privacy, Blaze," she responded, "but you are also a celebrity and there are people out there who want to know all the intimate details of your life. You and Livi do not have to go public with your marriage. However, the media is not going to let it go—not until the next big juicy story comes along."

Barbara rose to her feet. "I want to hear more about your time in Las Vegas, but let's do it over breakfast."

Blaze grabbed Livi's arm, holding her back. "I can't believe you would come all the way out here. Just because you have my last name does not make you a part of this family."

She snatched her arm away. "Keep your hands off me."

"I'm sorry," he said. "I didn't mean to hurt you. Livi, you have no right to be here."

"Ari and your parents thought otherwise."

"Instead of fighting each other, you two need to come together," Barbara suggested from the doorway. "I have a strong suspicion that Harold is behind this somehow. I wouldn't be surprised if he is having us followed by detectives."

"I'm not a fan of Harold's, but I doubt he had anything to do with this," Blaze said as he stepped around his mother to enter the dining room.

Barbara glanced at Livi and said, "Come, dear."

Livi sat down beside Blaze, but only because it was the only empty seat.

"Your son would rather believe that I am the one behind all this," Livi blurted. "Mrs. Alexander, you wanted to know how Blaze and I got together—well, I'll tell you. When we met, I thought he was intelligent, handsome and someone I wanted to get to know better. He seemed like a perfect gentleman." She paused a moment before continuing. "I loved the sound of his laughter and his sense of humor. We had a great time together."

Barbara smiled. "What about you, Blaze? What attracted you to Livi?"

"Everything about her," he responded. "We really clicked and I enjoyed being with her. She's right. We had a good time."

"So you two got married," Malcolm interjected.

"Apparently so," Blaze muttered.

Barbara took a sip of her herbal tea. "Marriage is a serious step and should not be taken lightly or made in mockery."

Blaze met his mother's gaze. "I know that, Mom."

"What happens now?" Malcolm asked.

"The only thing I know is that Livi hasn't been honest with me."

Barbara looked over at Livi and asked, "Do you agree?"

"Mrs. Alexander, I was wrong for not coming forward sooner. As for our marriage, I have strong feelings for Blaze. I thought he felt the same way about me. Vegas was romantic and everything was perfect between us. We just got caught up in the moment and I—"

"An annulment is the right thing to do," Blaze interjected, cutting her off. "What happened that night in Vegas was a mistake."

"I'm not sure your wife agrees," Malcolm stated.

"Don't forget that she walked out on our so-called marriage," Blaze stated coldly. "I think a lawyer would consider that abandonment."

Livi could not summon up an appetite. She could feel the tension permeating the room and was saddened by it.

"You're not eating," Blaze said quietly. A sudden thin chill hung on the edge of his words. "Your first *family* breakfast—I thought you'd be thrilled."

Livi permitted herself a withering stare. "I'm not hungry."

"Blaze, will you please stop being so rude," Sage blurted out. "Regardless of how it happened, Livi is your wife and you need to respect her as such."

He glared at his sister. "Why don't you focus on your own marriage and stay out of mine?"

"When did you become such a jerk?" Sage asked.

Livi rushed to her feet. "I can't do this," she said. "I will not have all of you fighting because of what happened. Blaze, I will sign whatever you need me to sign. I…I just need to get out of here. I'm sorry."

Blaze glanced over at his mother, who said, "You need to go after her."

He walked outside to the patio.

Livi was standing by the pool, wiping her eyes.

"You may have my family convinced that you're innocent with that little act of yours, but not me. What is it you want? Money?"

Her temper flared and Livi clenched her hands into fists. "You have some nerve."

He opened his mouth to speak, but before any words came out, she pushed him into the pool.

Zaire was the first one on the patio. She burst into laughter when she saw Blaze, soaking wet, getting out of the pool. "That's just what you deserve."

The rest of the family joined them.

Blaze stood there looking like a wet rag while his family laughed. The only person not laughing was Livi. She was crying.

She wiped her eyes. "I don't know how I could ever have fallen in love with you. I don't even want to be in the same room with you."

Livi turned to Malcolm and Barbara. "I'm not sorry for pushing him into the pool. He deserved it. I am sorry for ruining your breakfast. I didn't want to come because I had a feeling it would cause drama. I was right. I'm going to call for a taxi and wait out front."

Ari tossed Blaze a towel.

"You don't have to do that," Natasha said. "I'll drive you back. Ari can ride back with Sage and Ryan."

"Oh, yeah," Livi muttered as she pulled the newspaper out of her purse. "You need to see this," she stated, handing Blaze the tabloid.

He scanned it. "It's a picture of us the night we met for dinner."

"Right," she responded. "If I were the person responsible, then how did I get this photo snapped of us?" Livi pointed out. "Somebody had to have been there at the restaurant."

"Someone you told that we would be there," Blaze countered.

Livi glared at him.

"So you want me to believe that someone just happened to be there when we showed up and they recognized me?"

"They were either there already or came in after us. They saw us together and probably started researching me."

"I'm not buying it," Blaze stated with a shake of his head. "I have been under the radar since moving out here—why would they dig into my past to find dirt on me now? That doesn't make much sense."

"Blaze, you've made it perfectly clear that you don't want to be married to me," Livi snapped. "Let's just get this over and done with." She pulled out her cell phone.

"Who are you calling?"

"A taxi."

Minutes later, Livi ended the call and then said, "You will get your annulment. And do me a favor. Just stay as far away from me as possible."

"Blaze, you did not handle this situation very well," Malcolm said when his son came downstairs after changing into dry clothes.

"Livi is trying to play us," he responded angrily. "She had to be the one to leak news of our marriage. Dad, it could only be her."

"I'm not so sure. Anyone intent on finding dirt on this family could have come across your marriage license."

"Why do you believe so strongly in Livi's innocence?" Blaze asked. "What do we really know about her?"

"This girl is in love with you and I do not believe she would do anything to hurt you—especially something like this."

"She's not in love with me," Blaze argued. "Maybe she's in love with your money."

"Do you really believe that, son?" Barbara asked from the doorway. "Because I don't think you do. I believe that you care deeply for Livi."

He did not respond.

"I'm in the mood for a walk on the beach. Why don't you join me?"

Blaze smiled and nodded. "Sure, Mom."

They walked for a while without saying anything. Finally, Blaze said, "I know you didn't just want to take a morning stroll on the beach with me. What is it, Mom?"

"Now that Livi's gone, I'd like to know what your feelings are for this girl. Be honest with yourself."

"I was crazy about Livi," Blaze admitted. "I guess I still am, but I don't trust her any longer. She betrayed me."

"Hon, I know you believe that she did this, but I don't think so," Barbara stated. "I can see it in her face that she loves you. She does not want to end the marriage."

"Maybe that's why she decided to go public," Blaze

responded. "Maybe Livi thought this would buy her some time."

"I hadn't considered that possibility," Barbara said. "But I still do not think that Livi is the one responsible for this. She has too much to lose. Remember, she kept this secret for two years."

"We are not staying married," Blaze stated. "It would be a huge mistake."

She patted his arm. "Son, I know you're angry right now, but I want you to give yourself some time. You have already been married two years—why are you in such a hurry to put an end to it now?" Barbara inquired. "Have you met someone else?"

Blaze shook his head no. "There is no one else. Mom, I just want to go on with my life. I don't feel as if I can until this marriage is annulled."

"Have you considered making the marriage work?"

He laughed harshly. "Do you really think I can trust Livi after all that's happened?"

"In my opinion, it has not yet been proven that you can't trust her."

"I suppose you think that Livi and I should give the marriage a chance," Blaze said dryly.

"You have already been married to this girl for almost two years. I don't understand why you're in such a rush, especially if there is no other woman in the picture and you've admitted that you have feelings for her."

"Mom, have you considered that I just want to be a single man with no ties to anyone?"

Barbara sighed softly. "I never thought you would take marriage so lightly."

"I don't even remember the ceremony."

"There was something about Livi that prompted the

idea of marriage, whether you remember it or not. I just don't believe you should just let her walk out of your life like this. Love is always worth fighting for."

"I find her incredibly sexy and we have a good time together. I care a lot for Livi, but, to be honest, I have no idea why I married her so impulsively. I just don't remember."

Barbara shook her head. "I believe it was much more than that. Blaze, you have always been my wild child. You have turned out to be a wonderful man and I'm very proud of you."

"I don't want to ever disappoint you and Dad again," Blaze told her.

"We just want you to be happy, son. Livi is a sweet girl and she loves you so much. Sometimes it's better to be with someone who loves you, than being with someone you love."

Blaze considered his mother's words. He knew that she wanted him to at least give his marriage a shot. And he wanted to honor her wishes.

Chapter 15

"I've never seen this side of Blaze before," Natasha was saying. She had come to Livi's place a couple of hours later after leaving the Alexander estate. "Livi, I'm so sorry."

"It's not your fault. He's really angry with me for a lot of things," she said as she tossed a sweater into the suitcase lying open on her bed. "I didn't tell him I was in town and then I didn't tell him about the marriage. I never contacted the media, but Blaze is never going to believe me. We're over before we ever had a chance to start."

"You do love him."

Livi eyed her friend. "I think I've loved him from the moment we met. I know he's upset right now, but I never thought he would treat me this way."

"He's going to come around," Natasha assured Livi. "Blaze is a very private man."

Livi's eyes filled with tears.

She was heartbroken, but she would find a way to move on. She had known from the beginning that there was a chance that she and Blaze would not be together, but Livi held on to hope. Now that hope was completely gone. It had been destroyed by Blaze's lack of faith in her.

"Why are you leaving?" Natasha asked.

"I've been summoned by my parents. I had to call them this morning."

"How did they take it?"

"They're concerned," Livi stated. "Besides, I need to take some time just to deal with everything."

"You're coming back?" Natasha asked. "Right?"

Livi nodded. "I'm only going to be gone a couple of days."

When Natasha left, she finished packing her bag.

Before heading to the airport, Livi stopped by the boutique to speak with her staff. She had arranged for a short meeting.

When Livi walked into the boutique, her employees gathered around her.

"I'm sure all of you have heard the news by now and it's true," Livi announced. "Blaze and I are married. We have been married almost two years now. This is all that I am going to say on this matter right now, so let's get back to work. Also, if you are approached by any members of the media, I would like to think that your only response will be 'No comment.'"

Sybil and Amy arrived to take her to the airport.

"How are you holding up?" Amy asked.

"I'm fine," she responded.

"I called earlier and I was told that you were whisked away by Ari and his wife."

"There was a family meeting," Livi stated. "I was told that I was expected to attend, as well. It was about the marriage and how to deal with the media."

"I suppose Blaze was there," Amy said. "How did that go?"

"He was a first-class jerk and I ended up pushing him into the swimming pool."

Sybil and Amy laughed.

"I shouldn't have done it, but Blaze was just getting on my nerves. I never thought he could be so mean."

"Say good riddance," Amy said. "But make sure that you consult an attorney before you sign anything."

Livi could tell that Amy was about to launch into a tirade about men. She had just gone through a bitter divorce and had nothing good to say about men these days.

It was a short flight to San Francisco. Much too short, as far as Livi was concerned. This was one of those rare occasions when she was not looking forward to seeing her parents.

Livi walked briskly through Baggage Claim with her carry-on and headed straight to the gleaming stretch limousine waiting at the curb.

The chauffeur greeted her with a smile. "It is good to see you, Miss Olson."

"It's nice seeing you, too, Ralph."

Pacific Heights had the widespread reputation as San Francisco's most luxurious neighborhood, but Livi disagreed. In her opinion, the small patch of land hidden between the Presidio, Lincoln Park and the ocean, called Sea Cliff, ranked as the city's most exclusive piece of real estate. After all, her parents would only settle for the very best.

The limo pulled into the circular driveway of a sprawling Mediterranean-style villa perched above the Pacific.

She inhaled deeply and then exhaled slowly.

Livi walked into the house.

Her parents were waiting for her in the formal living room. She embraced them both before taking a seat on the custom-designed sectional sofa.

Her mother spoke first. "I'm a bit confused. I thought you had the marriage annulled two years ago."

"That's what you wanted me to do, Mother. It was not what I wanted."

"We've allowed you to live your life as you chose, Elizabeth. We did as you asked and did not interfere, but now in the wake of what's happened, your mother and I would like to help you sort this out."

"Daddy, this is my problem and I'll work it out."

"You never told us that you were married to Robert DePaul's grandson," her mother interjected.

"I didn't know it at the time," Livi responded with a sigh. "What does it matter?"

"Do you love him?"

Livi looked at her mother. "Yes, I do. But we are not going to stay married. According to Blaze, it was a mistake."

"I wouldn't dismiss your marriage so easily," her mother interjected. "After all, you are married to one of the heirs to Robert DePaul's estate."

"Is that all you can think about, Mother? I could care less about Blaze being an heir to anything."

"Darling, you have always been such a romantic. Your father and I married because our parents wished it, and it has been a good marriage." She looked at her husband. "Wouldn't you agree?"

Both of her parents had come from money and their marriage united two cosmetics companies into one successful conglomerate that was worth billions. Marriage without love may have worked for her parents, but this was not what Livi wanted for herself.

There was no way she would stay married to Blaze if he did not love her.

"I think the first plan of action is for us to meet your husband and his family," her mother was saying.

Livi shook her head. "No way. I made this mess and I'll take care of it myself."

Her mother opened her mouth to argue, but Livi held up a hand. "I mean it. I am going to take care of this situation myself. There is no way I'm going to let you try to form some type of merger with the Alexander-DePaul Hotel Group. Besides, Blaze has no idea who I really am—I need time to fix all this before he can ever meet you and Daddy."

"Why do you insist on all this secrecy?" her father asked. "Are you ashamed to be an Olson? It's a good name."

"I want people to get to know me and not who my parents are."

Franklin walked out onto the patio where Blaze was seated.

"May I join you?" he asked.

"Sure," Blaze responded. For the past couple of days, Blaze had spent most of his time in a chair near the pool.

They sat together in silence for a moment.

"Do you think that Livi did this, Franklin? I never thought she would betray me in this way."

"Livi would never speak to the media about her private life."

Blaze looked at him. "How can you be so sure?"

"Because I know her," Franklin responded. "You've heard of Olson Cosmetics?"

Frowning in confusion, Blaze responded, "I guess. Wait...yeah, I've heard of the company. What about it?"

"Livi's full name is Elizabeth Carlyle Olson," Franklin announced.

Blaze's eyes rose in surprise. "Are you saying that Livi is Olson Cosmetics?"

"Her parents own the company," Franklin stated. "She is an heiress to a billion-dollar company."

Blaze was stunned. "She never mentioned that."

"She wouldn't. At least not right away. Livi is much like you when it comes to her privacy and living a normal life. She wanted to make sure any man she was involved with dated her because she was just Livi."

"She's definitely not after my father's money," Blaze said. "I was wrong about that."

He couldn't help but wonder what else he might be wrong about.

"How do I make this right?" he asked Franklin.

"I have a feeling that an apology may be a good place to start."

"I said some horrible things to her."

"If you care for her, then go after her." Franklin rose to his feet. "I have to pack. I'm flying with your father to Arizona in a few hours."

Blaze nodded. "Thanks."

He stayed outside for another hour, silently considering Franklin's advice.

When he walked into the house, he spotted his father in the kitchen with his mother. Blaze stood there watching them as they embraced and kissed. It was not unusual for him to catch his parents displaying affection openly.

He cleared his throat loudly. "C'mon, you two. Give your son a break."

Barbara walked over and patted his cheek. "Why don't you try to call Livi?"

"I think I was wrong about her," Blaze said. "She probably hates me now."

His mother shook her head. "I doubt that. I'm sure Livi's hurt and upset, but it's not something you can't fix, if this is what you really have a mind to do."

"Mom, what do you think I should do?"

"I think you and Livi need to talk to each other," Barbara stated. She reached out and took Malcolm's hand in hers. "Marriage is sacred, son. Although this may not have been the ideal situation for you and Livi, I wouldn't just walk away without seeing if something is there."

Malcolm wrapped his arms around his wife. "I agree with your mother. I know you care for your wife. Isn't that worth fighting for?"

"There's something else," Blaze announced. "Livi's parents own Olson Cosmetics."

Barbara's mouth opened and closed in shock. "Really?"

"She's not after your money, Dad."

Malcolm laughed. "I never thought she was."

"I think I'll fly down to Aspen for a few days," Blaze

announced. "I need to get away and think about everything."

"Son, I think that's a great idea," Malcolm stated. "You've got quite a bit to consider."

Chapter 16

Four days passed since Livi's return home, and she had not heard a word from Blaze. As far as she knew, Blaze had not come near the hotel and she had heard that he had not been in the office, either. Supposedly, he was away on a business trip, but Livi believed otherwise.

Livi missed hearing his voice and that sexy laughter that warmed her all over.

Regardless, he had left her back here to deal with the fallout. Livi had changed her home number, and Ari arranged for the store to have security posted to keep reporters out. However, every now and then, she felt as if she were being watched.

At work, the other employees treated her differently. In their minds, she was an Alexander.

If they only knew.

Livi decided to work until closing, since there was

no reason for her to rush home. She did not want to hear Sybil's constant advice to seek alimony from Blaze. She did not want anything but his heart and if she couldn't have that…

Livi felt her eyes water.

I'm not going to cry. I'm not.

She did not make it home until shortly after ten.

"Sybil," she called out.

There was no response.

Livi was glad to have the condo to herself. She was tired and she did not feel like talking.

She ran a hot bath and undressed.

Livi stepped into the tub and sat down to soak in the bubbly water. She leaned back and closed her eyes.

She stayed in the tub until the water began to cool.

Livi got out, dried off and then slipped on a pair of silk pajamas. She grabbed a novel and walked into the living room to sit down and read for a while before going to bed.

There was a knock on her door.

"Sybil, where is your key? I—" Livi stopped short at the sight of Blaze standing there.

"I'm sorry for coming by so late, but I really need to see you."

"I don't want to see you," Livi stated.

"Please, I want to apologize for my actions."

"Some things you cannot apologize for, Blaze." Livi was about to close the door, but his foot prevented her from slamming the door in his face. "We have nothing to talk about."

"We have a lot to discuss," Blaze countered. "Including your connection to Olson Cosmetics. Please let me in."

Livi's eyes registered surprise, but it was gone as quickly as it had come. "It's late, Blaze, and I really don't feel like arguing."

"That's not why I'm here. Livi, I just want a chance to make this right between us."

She met his gaze. "Why? Did you find out who told the tabloids about our marriage? I'm sure you've done some investigating."

"I know that it wasn't you, but no. I haven't found out anything concrete."

"I guess this sudden change in your attitude has to do with the fact that my last name is Olson." Livi shook her head sadly. "Goodbye, Blaze."

"Livi…"

"No," she interjected. "We are done. Now move your foot or lose it."

"Good night," he said, then turned and walked away.

Livi resisted the urge to call him back. She had to stand her ground. He had hurt her and she was not about to just let him back into her life to do more damage.

Blaze had not expected a warm welcome, but he had expected to at least get past the door. Livi was furious with him and, truth be told, he couldn't really blame her.

While in Aspen, he'd had a lot of time to think about his relationship with Livi. He felt like a piece of his heart was missing.

Blaze was not sure if what he felt was love, but it was probably as close to it as he'd felt for any woman. He didn't care about her wealth and understood why she had chosen to distance herself from it. Blaze probably would have chosen that route had the opportunity presented itself.

Livi had declared her love for him. Maybe his parents were right. He owed it to himself to explore his relationship further. He had a wife and now the whole world knew it.

The next day, Livi arrived at work and saw two dozen red roses on the counter near the register.

"These just came for you," Martha announced. "I'm pretty sure they are from that handsome husband of yours."

Livi read the note and smiled.

I've handled this whole situation badly from the very beginning. I'm sorry for being a jerk and would really like a second chance. Please consider moving in with me. We owe it to ourselves to see if what we have is real.
Blaze

"What did I tell you?" Martha said with a grin.

Livi inhaled the fragrance of the bouquet. "They are beautiful."

Martha agreed. "If I were you, I'd head to my office and make a phone call to a certain someone."

"I don't know…"

"Call him," Martha urged.

Livi walked back to her office and picked up the phone.

When Blaze answered, she said, "Thank you for the flowers and the invitation. The roses are beautiful."

"I've gone about all of this the wrong way and I've been a jerk. Livi, I hope you can believe that I never wanted to hurt you. I just let my anger get the better of me."

"I don't want to dwell on the past or stay angry with you, Blaze. Thanks for the flowers and I appreciate the apology."

"Did you mean what you said to me?" he asked. "Are you in love with me?"

"It doesn't matter anymore," Livi responded.

"Please, I'd like to know."

"Yes, I do love you, Blaze."

"I didn't know."

"As I said, it really doesn't matter, Blaze. Have you started the process of obtaining the annulment?"

"That's why I wanted to talk to you, Livi. I thought about it some more, and I think that maybe we should try to see if we can be together."

Livi stared at the phone, and then put it back to her ear. "What did you just say?"

"I want you in my life."

She was speechless.

"Livi..." Blaze prompted.

"I'm here. I'm just in shock right now."

"I can't get you out of my mind. Believe me, I've tried."

"So what are you really saying to me?" Livi asked.

"I want to try to make our marriage work," Blaze announced. "I want to be your husband."

"Don't play games with me," Livi snapped. "This is totally not funny."

"Honey, it's not meant to be. I'm serious. I thought about everything you've said and what my mother told me. Marriage is sacred and should be treated as such.

However, we can't have a marriage if we don't try to build on what we have."

"So are you saying that you want us together as in living together as a married couple?" Livi asked. She wanted to be sure she was clear on what Blaze was saying.

"Yeah. I would like for you to move in with me."

"Why the sudden change of heart?"

"Because I care deeply for you, Livi. I want to see where this thing between us goes."

"Can we discuss this later tonight?" she asked. "I need some time to digest this turn of events."

Chapter 17

They were seated in a booth in La Parrilla having dinner.

"Why didn't you tell me who you really were?" he asked Livi.

She wiped her mouth on the edge of her napkin. "I wanted you to love me for me. I didn't want it to be about my parents' money. I told you that we had a lot in common."

"Are there any more secrets?" Blaze wanted to know.

Livi noticed his set face and clamped mouth. "No, you know them all now."

"I'm truly sorry for the way I acted, Livi. I was thrown by the news of our marriage, but I should have handled it differently."

"We both made mistakes, but I would like to wipe the slate clean," she responded.

Blaze reached over and took her hand in his own. "I'd like for us to start over."

A delicious shudder heated her body at his touch. Livi felt the heat of desire wash over her like waves. Her eyes traveled to his lips. She wanted so much to feel the touch of his mouth against hers. Livi cleared her throat, pretending not to be affected by Blaze. "I'd like that, too."

Blaze seemed to be staring at her intently.

She broke into a tiny smile. "You're doing it again."

"Doing what?"

"Staring at me."

"I love looking at you," Blaze admitted. "I happen to find you incredibly beautiful."

The waiter's appearance with their dinner put a temporary block on their conversation.

So far, the evening was going quite well, Livi acknowledged.

From the moment Blaze arrived at her door, he openly admired the way she looked for their date and had complimented her several times throughout dinner on her dress.

Livi silently noted how handsome Blaze looked in his gray suit. She was totally entranced by him.

"Eventually, the connection to my parents will come out," Livi said after taking a sip of her iced tea. "With any luck, another more high-profile celebrity will get into trouble and we'll be old news."

"How did they take the news?" Blaze inquired.

"They couldn't be happier," Livi said. "But, unfortunately, they view our marriage as a potential business merger of some kind."

Blaze laughed. "My family really likes you. For yourself. It's not about money or any type of merger."

She looked at him. "Are you sure?"

He nodded.

Barbara had greatly influenced Blaze's decision to stay in his marriage. He could not bear disappointing her again, which is why he decided to do as she suggested. Blaze had not lied to Livi, but he was not about to tell her they were getting together because his mother wanted them to.

"Blaze, are you sure about our moving in together? Before everything came out, you wanted to just take it one day at a time."

"I didn't know I already had a wife at the time."

"So you want to give our marriage a chance?" Livi studied the expression on his face.

"Yes," he responded. "I want to try to see if we can make this work."

She smiled. "Thank you, Blaze."

They left the restaurant and drove to Livi's place. She made a pot of coffee, and then sat down with Blaze in the living room.

"I'm still having trouble believing that you want to stay married," she confessed.

Blaze reached over, drawing her closer to him. He seemed to read her thoughts because he held her in his arms while kissing her passionately.

When Blaze pulled away, he said, "We have something special together, sweetheart. It took me a while, but I've finally realized it."

In response, Livi pulled his head down to hers. Their lips met and she felt buffeted by the winds of a savage harmony. Her senses reeled as if short-circuited and made her knees tremble.

Breaking their kiss, Livi buried her face against Blaze's throat. Her trembling limbs clung to him helplessly. She was extremely conscious of where his warm flesh made contact with hers.

Blaze touched a finger to her chin. His eyes were bright with an emotion she could not identify.

His mouth curved up at the corners. His finger brushed against her skin, moving back and forth, making it difficult to think.

Desire ignited in her belly, causing her to pull away reluctantly.

"What's wrong, sweetheart?"

"Nothing. I just don't think it's a good idea for us to get carried away," she murmured against his cheek.

Blaze pulled her back into his arms. He gazed into her eyes.

Livi drew his face to hers in a renewed embrace.

He kissed her again, lingering, savoring every moment.

Her emotions whirled. Blood pounded in her brain, leapt from her heart and made her knees tremble.

She rose to her feet and held her hand out to Blaze.

"I don't want you to leave, but I also do not want to make love. It's too soon for me after all that's happened."

Blaze nodded in understanding.

She and Blaze climbed in bed and lay on top of the covers. He held her in his arms, keeping her close to him.

"Thank you," he whispered.

"For what?"

"For giving me a second chance."

Livi turned in his arms to face him. "You mean the world to me, Blaze. I want your trust and your love. I don't need anything else."

He kissed her. "I have your love and I want to earn back your faith in me. Right before you pushed me into the pool, I saw the expression on your face. I never want you to look at me in that way again. You were so hurt."

"Let's not look back, Blaze. Let's just focus on what we have—the future."

Livi moved in with Blaze the following weekend. She was excited about them starting their life together as husband and wife. Blaze seemed to feel the same way.

He had taken care of everything, from having her things packed up to scheduling the movers. He had even had his housekeeper unpack everything except her clothing.

"Wow, there's hardly anything left for me to do," she said, glancing around.

Livi had just gotten off work and this was the first day of living in her new home. It was also the first time she was there since the night of Malcolm's party.

Blaze wasn't there when she arrived. It felt strange being there without him.

This is my home, too, she reminded herself.

Livi strolled into the vast gourmet-style kitchen to see what she had to work with. She wanted to have dinner prepared by the time Blaze came home.

She smiled when she noted how everything was organized and stacked neatly in the drawers and chocolate-colored cabinets. This was something else that she and Blaze had in common. They were both very organized.

The collection of vintage car models on the bookshelves at the end of the island brought a smile to Livi's lips. The subzero refrigerator was fully stocked with a variety of meats, produce and dairy products.

She decided on steaks and roasted potatoes for dinner.

Livi washed the meat and potatoes in the stainless-steel sink before placing them on a wooden platter. She prepared and seasoned the meat for grilling first. Next, she wrapped the potatoes in foil and stuck them in the oven.

Livi had just taken the steaks off the grill when Blaze walked through the door. He greeted her with a warm smile. "Honey, I'm home."

She laughed.

He strode into the kitchen and kissed her. "Seriously, I'm home."

Livi wrapped her arms around him and they kissed passionately. "I am, too."

"Dinner smells delicious."

"Why don't you go get comfortable and I'll get plates and take them to the dining room?" Livi suggested.

Blaze kissed her again before leaving the kitchen.

Livi smiled to herself. Things were getting off to a great start.

She was seated at the table when Blaze returned wearing a pair of sweats and a Lakers T-shirt.

He sat down across from her.

"How was your day?" Livi inquired.

"Pretty good," Blaze responded as he placed a linen napkin on his lap. "I was in meetings most of the day."

"My staff is still acting like I'm a stranger. I know that they must feel as if I betrayed them in some way. I've heard that some of my coworkers have accused me of being a spy for your family."

Blaze laughed. "Seriously?"

Livi nodded. "I wish everyone would just focus on their own lives."

"So do I."

"I don't understand why everyone feels we owe them an explanation."

"We don't, Livi."

"I love my job, but when I'm there..."

"You do not have to work at all, Livi. In fact, my dad and I were talking about your becoming the centralized buyer for all the boutiques. You've done a great job with Parisian Maison."

"Really?"

Blaze nodded. "I think it's the way to go. We can cut down expenses by having one person doing the buying for the whole chain. Of course, we have considered having a couple of assistant buyers work with you."

"Will I be able to select my assistants?" Livi wanted to know.

"Yes, of course. We'll have a formal meeting at the end of the week."

"Great. I've been saying that we need a corporate buyer for the past year or so."

"My father mentioned it a few months ago and we decided to do some research. After reviewing all the reports and talking with Natasha, we all decided it's a good move. However, this means that you will be working in the corporate offices from now on."

"So does this mean we'll be carpooling?" Livi asked with a grin.

"Definitely."

Later in the evening, Livi and Blaze settled down on the sofa to watch television.

Her eyes strayed to the door of the master bedroom. Biting her lip, Livi looked away.

"We don't have to do anything until you're ready,"

he said in a low voice. "I'm willing to take it just one day at a time."

She loved Blaze with her entire being. He was so compelling, his magnetism so potent. Whenever he held her, she could feel his heart thudding against her own. There were times, when he was standing near her, that Livi could feel the heat emanating from his body. Blaze's actions told her more than he could ever put into words.

Chapter 18

Guilt snaked down Blaze's spine every time Livi expressed her love for him. He wished that he could return the sentiment—mostly because he knew Livi wanted him to, but to do so would be a lie.

There were days when he thought what he was feeling for her might be love, but then at other times, he reasoned that it was just a kinship. She made no demands on him. She was pretty much a free spirit and very independent.

Livi stretched and yawned.

"Are you ready to go to bed?" he asked.

She boldly met his gaze. "Yes, I think I am."

He rose to his feet. "After you."

Livi took him by the hand and led him to the master bedroom.

Standing outside the door, Blaze asked, "Are you sure? I can sleep in one of the guestrooms."

"We can't have a real marriage in separate bedrooms, Blaze. I'm not saying that we should make love. But if we do, I want it to happen naturally."

As soon as they entered the bedroom, Blaze pulled Livi into his embrace. "I want to be your husband in every way," he whispered in a voice choked with passion. "I'll wait until you're ready. I meant that, but I want you to know how much I want to make love to you."

Livi placed a hand to his cheek. "I have to be honest with you. Blaze, I'm struggling, as well. I just think it's too soon. I want you in the same room with me, but I'll understand if you—"

"No," Blaze interjected. "I can control my urges, sweetheart. I want to wake up beside you." He stepped forward and clasped her body tightly to his.

Explosive currents raced through Livi.

She eased away from Blaze. "I'm going to take a shower."

He groaned. "Now you're going to torture me with the image of you with water dripping off that sexy body of yours."

Livi kissed his cheek. "I'll see you in a few minutes, husband."

The next day when Livi arrived at work, she was met by one of her employees.

"We found it stuck in the door," Martha said. "Livi, I want you to know that I don't believe that trash."

Confused, she asked, "What are you talking about?"

Livi glanced down at the tabloid and gasped.

She pulled her keys out of her purse and headed toward the door.

"Livi…" Martha called out.

"I have to go," she said. "I'll be back, but right now I need to go see Blaze."

Livi drove to the corporate headquarters and walked straight to her husband's office.

She thrust the tabloid at him. "Do you know what they are saying about me? I've been depicted as some gold digger who married you for your money. Supposedly some secret source has confirmed that I knew what was in Robert's will and sought you out."

Blaze was stunned. "What?"

"This anonymous source sounds almost as vindictive as Harold DePaul," Livi snapped. "If Harold really did this, then I promise you one thing. He's going to regret the day he ever met me by the time I'm through with him."

"This does sound like Harold."

"I see I stopped by just in time."

Livi and Blaze both turned toward the door.

Harold held up both hands as if to ward off an attack. "I had nothing to do with any of this."

"I don't believe you," Blaze uttered. "This whole things smells of you."

"Really? Well, I heard that you thought it was your lovely wife who spilled the beans."

"What are you doing here?"

"I came to make sure you know who is responsible for all of this. It's not me, but I know who it is. He came to me, and I thought I'd purchased all the photographs, but apparently not."

"How long have you known about our marriage?" Livi asked.

"For a while," Harold responded. "I hate seeing you

so upset, Livi. I consider you a friend and I never would do something like this to you."

"Who is responsible?" Blaze wanted to know.

"He's a private detective. His name is George Pepper and he used to work for me from time to time. He was at the restaurant in the booth behind you and overheard a conversation that made him curious, so he decided to do some investigating on his own."

"Why did you pay him for the pictures?" Livi asked.

"I didn't want them published. Apparently, I didn't offer George enough money. He sold the story to the highest bidder."

"Why should I believe you?" Blaze asked Harold.

"Because I'm here." He handed a packet to Blaze. "These are the pictures I bought from George. I'd told him not to discuss anything he had learned about you and Livi. I thought he would keep his word." Harold paused a heartbeat, and then said, "However, there is something else that you two need to know. I did some checking of my own and, as it turns out, you two are not really married."

"What are you talking about?" Blaze demanded. "We have a marriage certificate that proves otherwise."

"Harold," Livi prompted.

"The preacher who married you…well, he wasn't licensed. Your marriage is not valid."

"I don't believe you," Livi said. "Harold, why do you have to be so cruel?"

"I'm telling you the truth. You can check for yourselves."

Harold made his way to the door. "I just thought you should know."

When Harold left, Blaze turned to Livi and asked, "Do you believe him?"

"I don't know."

Blaze met her gaze. "Livi, we'll check it out."

She sank down in a nearby chair. "All this time, I thought we were married. Our wedding anniversary is tomorrow."

"We are still going to celebrate our anniversary."

Livi shook her head. "I don't think we should. Especially if we're not really married."

Blaze pushed away from his desk. He walked around to where Livi was sitting. "Everything is going to be fine."

"First, I have to deal with tabloids saying that I'm a gold digger and now this." Livi chewed on her bottom lip. "Blaze, I would never do anything to hurt you or your family. I hope you will remember this in the future."

"Hopefully, all the rumors and gossip will die down soon. I know it upsets you, but try to ignore it."

Livi chewed on her bottom lip. "I'm finding that's a lot easier said than done."

Today was their second anniversary.

Livi eyed the dining-room table and smiled. She had scented candles placed around the room and in the center of the table.

I really want this evening to be perfect.

Humming softly, Livi strolled into the kitchen to see how her meal was faring. Her lobster bisque had been in the slow cooker since she left for work. She opened the oven to check on the seafood casserole.

Livi left the kitchen and went upstairs to put on a

strapless maxi dress. She then slipped on a pair of bejeweled sandals.

Blaze arrived thirty minutes later with a huge bouquet of flowers.

"Something smells good," he told her when she stepped aside to let him enter the condo.

"Thank you," she said with a smile. "Everything should be ready soon."

"These are for you," Blaze said, holding out the flowers to her. "When I saw them, they reminded me of you. I remember how much you admired these when you saw them displayed around the hotel lobby in Las Vegas."

She sniffed the colorful bouquet and said, "They're beautiful, Blaze. I'm touched that you remembered."

Blaze and Livi sat down at the dining table.

He blessed the food and asked God to watch over their marriage.

Livi could feel Blaze watching her. "Shouldn't you be concentrating on your food?" She was eager for him to try the seafood casserole she'd prepared for the first time ever in her life. Livi was curious to see if it turned out well, and was to her husband's liking.

Blaze's eyes traveled over her face, and then slid downward. "When I saw you in Vegas, I thought you were an illusion. I could not believe that you really existed. I had never seen anyone so beautiful. Then, as I got to know you, I realized what an amazing woman you are. What I'm trying to say is that I'm a very lucky man."

She took a sip of her lemonade. "My first impression of you was that you were a ladies' man. I didn't want to have anything to do with you. I saw the way your frat brothers were ogling the women, but then I noticed that you kind of stayed to yourself. Then I thought that you had to be married."

He laughed. "That's why you checked my left hand when I asked you to dance?"

"Yes," Livi responded with a chuckle.

"Did I propose to you?" Blaze asked.

She looked at him. "Not exactly. We were having lunch and this couple walked in. It was clear that they had gotten married. We started talking about marriage and you mentioned being married to your work. Somehow, the subject turned to you and me getting married."

"So we just did it?"

"We talked about it at length," Livi responded. "I was going to move to Atlanta to start our lives as husband and wife. You told me that you loved me and that everything about us felt right."

"You never told me this part," Blaze said.

"I didn't think you were ready to hear it. I don't know if you can imagine how much it hurt to hear you tell your frat brothers that you cared for me, but that you had no interest in being married to me. It broke my heart."

"I'm sorry."

Livi met his gaze. "You didn't know. I understand that now."

Blaze met her gaze straight on. "Despite the crazy way our marriage began, I can't see my life without you in it, Livi."

She wiped her mouth with the edge of her napkin. "I feel the same way."

"My favorite moment in Vegas is the night we danced in the rain," Blaze said. "That's the moment I knew our relationship changed."

Livi agreed. "It's when I knew that I didn't want to leave what we had in Vegas behind."

He tasted the casserole. "This is delicious."

She smiled. "Thank you."

Once they were done eating, they put the dishes into the dishwasher and put away the rest of the food. When the kitchen was clean, they settled down in the living room.

Blaze pulled her into his arms, holding her close.

"I have something for you," he said, planting a kiss on her forehead.

Livi sat up. "What is it?"

He handed her a slim, gift-wrapped box.

Inside was a diamond necklace.

"It's gorgeous," she murmured.

Livi met his gaze. "I have something for you, too." She handed him a gift box that contained a watch. It was one Blaze had been admiring at the boutique.

He smiled when he saw it. "I thought you'd sold it when I didn't see it in the boutique anymore."

"I knew how much you loved it, so I thought it would make the perfect anniversary gift."

His mouth covered hers. She responded to his kiss as desire ignited in her belly. Livi felt as if she were losing herself in Blaze. It was as if the two of them were becoming one.

Turning in his arms, Livi lifted her mouth to him, kissing him softly. Unnamable sensations ran through her as Blaze's hands traveled down her body. She felt the heat from their closeness and the core of her began to burn with his touch.

Blaze gently grasped Livi's hand, his fingers fondling its smoothness. When she looked up at him, her gaze sent currents through him. "Being together like this feels so right."

Livi agreed as her emotions whirled.

Later, she and Blaze lay in bed with damp tangled sheets draped around them.

Chapter 19

The next day, Blaze and Livi drove to Pacific Palisades for a day of fun and grilling outside. With everyone seated around the Olympic-size pool, the conversation turned to basketball.

Livi proved that she was a perfect fit for the Alexander family when she stepped out on the basketball court with Natasha and Zaire. Blaze sat with Ari and the rest of his brothers to watch the women play.

"Go, Mommy," Joshua yelled.

"Livi has some skills," Ari said.

Blaze agreed. "Yeah, she does. Hey, should Natasha be out on the court like that?" He was worried about the fact that she was pregnant.

"She's holding back," Ari said. "Natasha says the doctor encourages exercise. I'm not sure he meant basketball, however."

Almost as if she'd heard them, Natasha walked off the court. "That's it for me."

Both Ari and Blaze released a sigh of relief.

Later, it was the men's turn to play.

Livi cheered for her husband. "Hey, how can you miss that, sweetie? C'mon, Blaze…"

Natasha laughed. "I have a feeling that Ari and I are both going to need to soak in the tub tonight. No more basketball for me until after I have this baby."

"I know what you mean," Livi said. "My body is so sore."

She was blissfully happy and the more time she spent with Blaze's family, the more she felt like a part of the family.

That evening, as she and Blaze lay in bed snuggling, Livi asked, "Have you heard anything from Ira?"

He nodded.

Livi sat up in bed. "What did he say?"

Blaze looked up at her and said, "The man who married us did not have a license to do so."

She felt as if a bucket of cold water had been splashed all over her.

He sat up and pulled her into his arms, kissing her.

A brief shiver rippled through Livi. She buried her face against the corded muscles of his chest. She had no desire to back out of his embrace. "I can't believe this. You're not really my husband." She started to cry.

He gazed down at her with tenderness. "It's only a piece of paper, honey. It doesn't change the way I feel about you. Nothing has to change."

Parting her lips, Livi raised herself to meet his kiss.

His lips pressed against hers, and then gently covered her mouth.

The kiss sent the pit of Livi's stomach into a wild swirl.

Blaze showered her with kisses around her lips and along her jaw. As he roused her passion, his own grew stronger.

They made love slowly at first, the rhythm gradually building to a frenzied pace. In bed, Blaze and Livi were truly united. They were one.

Ari and Blaze took the elevator to the executive suite at the Alexander DePaul Hotel in San Diego. They had driven down for a meeting and to tour the newest hotel in their chain. It was similar to the one in Beverly Hills but on a smaller scale.

Blaze noted the tastefully painted walls with a warm walnut trim, accompanied by a spectacular view of a lush botanical garden. "This décor is similar to the hotel in Phoenix," he said.

Ari agreed.

They sat down in one of the richly appointed conference rooms and waited for the others to arrive. Blaze openly admired the artwork displayed on gleaming, wood-paneled walls. He glanced up at the two enormous crystal chandeliers hanging above the table.

"I know these had to have cost a pretty penny," he said.

Ari followed his gaze and responded. "Oh, yeah…"

"I like the velvet drapes in here. They go well with the décor and the furnishings," he said. "I've given Livi the okay to make some changes to our place, so we've been watching a lot of HGTV."

Ari laughed. "Same here. Natasha is looking for inspiration for the nursery. I told her to just hire an interior decorator, but she wants it to be a family project."

Blaze eyed the appetizing presentation of delicacies for them to enjoy during their meeting.

"I don't know which one I like better," Blaze said. "This one or the property in Phoenix."

"My favorite is probably the one in Dallas."

"It's really nice," Blaze said. His eyes traveled the room, pausing briefly on the fifty-inch plasma TV. "I just bought one of those."

They continued to make small talk as they waited for the general manager and other members of the management team to arrive.

"The new campaign has been very successful..." Daniel Ewing, the general manager stated. "Our reports indicate a 13.5 percent surge in total room reservations sold in the three-month period from May to July. This is one of the best performances for some time, with occupancy levels the highest in five years."

Blaze scanned the information in front of him, but he could hardly focus. His mind was on Livi. He had only been gone a day and he found that he already missed her. These feelings were new to him.

He forced his attention back to the conversation at hand.

Ari was going over a laundry list of items that must have come from their father, Blaze surmised.

At the end of the day, Ari and Blaze hung out together in Ari's suite.

"Have you and Natasha found out the sex of the baby?"

Ari shook his head no. "We want to be surprised.

I think Ryan and Sage plan on finding out the sex of their baby, though."

"I would want to know," Blaze stated.

"Are you and Livi planning to start a family soon?"

"No, we're definitely not there yet."

Ari met his gaze. "Why would you say it like that? I thought things were great between the two of you."

"Things are good," Blaze acknowledged. "But we're not ready to bring a child into the relationship."

"Does Livi feel the same way you do?" Ari inquired. "Because I think she's ready to start a family. I overheard her and Natasha talking the other day."

Blaze put down his fork. "We haven't really talked about it. We're still trying to see if our marriage is viable."

Ari frowned. "I thought you two wanted to be together."

"That's what we're working toward."

"Blaze, do you love Livi?"

"Truth?"

Ari nodded.

"I don't know if I would call it love. I care for her and I enjoy being with her."

His brother gave him a disapproving look. "Livi doesn't deserve to be hurt."

"I know that," Blaze stated. "I don't intend to hurt her. I'm being the best husband I can be to her."

"But you don't love her."

"Maybe I will grow to love her."

Ari shook his head. "I don't know, bro. Maybe it was better to have gotten the annulment. If you don't handle this the right way, you're going to lose the best thing to ever happen to you."

"I know that in my head, but try telling that to my heart."

"She's a gorgeous woman. She's not going to sit around and wait for you forever."

Blaze did not respond.

It was late when Blaze got home. He found Livi sound asleep in their bedroom. He watched her for a moment before easing out of his clothes and climbing into bed with her. She had this tiny little smile tugging at her lips even as she slumbered.

Blaze kissed her lightly on the cheek.

Livi stirred but did not wake up.

He kissed her on her forehead and nuzzled her ear.

She stirred once more, this time moaning softly.

He lay down and placed a protective arm across Livi's waist, loving the way her body felt against his own.

They were a perfect fit.

His body responded to the silky feel of her skin against his.

Unconsciously, Livi snuggled against him, igniting a wave of desire within him.

Blaze tried to recall if he had ever been as happy as he was now. She turned in his arms, forcing his thoughts to the back of his mind.

He planted tiny kisses along her cheek and her neck to wake her up.

Livi moaned softly.

He continued his slow seduction.

Her passion aroused, Livi opened her eyes.

They soon connected in a sensual dance that lovers do, the union setting off fireworks that they both experienced.

Afterward, Blaze continued to hold her close as they slept, satiated from the fulfillment of desire.

She reached over and took his hand in hers. "I love you."

Her words were met with silence.

Chapter 20

Humming softly, Livi admired her new office in the corporate headquarters of the Alexander-DePaul Group. Her office was on the opposite end of the hall from Blaze's. It was not as large as his, but was decorated just as richly in mahogany tones. The paint on her walls was a soft dove-gray color.

She had come in over the weekend to hang pictures and add accessories that reflected her personal taste. This was a great job opportunity and Livi was thrilled. She knew there were those who believed she was given the job because she was married to Blaze, but Livi had her own professional standards to meet.

She sat down at her new desk. The first thing on her agenda was to check her email. Livi was expecting an email from a vendor with the new price list for the upcoming holiday season.

Blaze strode into her office with purpose. "I see that you're all settled in."

Livi broke into a smile. "I am."

"Good. If you're not too busy, I'd like to have lunch with my wife later this afternoon."

"I'm never too busy for you, Blaze."

He sat down in one of the visitor chairs facing her. "Sage and Ryan are supposed to find out the sex of the baby in a couple of weeks. I have never seen two people more excited."

"Having a baby is a joyous occasion."

Blaze met her gaze. "You do know that we're not ready for something like that?"

Livi's smile disappeared. "How would I know that? We haven't discussed having children."

"We're not ready to have a family. Our focus is on building a solid foundation for our marriage."

Livi pushed away from her desk and rose to her feet. She walked over to the window and stared out. "You do want children eventually, right?"

"Yes, I'd like to have a family, but not any time soon."

Livi chewed on her bottom lip.

"I guess this is a discussion we should have had earlier."

She turned around to face him and said, "That would have been nice."

"I haven't ruled out having a family, Livi. I just want our marriage on solid ground and right now it is still too fragile. I do not want my child raised in a broken home."

"Neither do I," Livi stated. "We will table the baby discussion until we decide when we are going to get married."

She thought she detected a flicker of something in Blaze's eyes, but she could not identify it.

When he left her office, Livi sat down at her desk and tried to focus on work, but every now and then, her mind drifted back to Blaze and their earlier conversation. It left her feeling uneasy, although she could not figure out why.

Her day was busy, but Livi had no problem keeping up with the pace. She had her new assistant order lunch for her from a nearby deli.

When the food arrived, Livi ate while she worked.

Livi stayed as busy as she could because she did not want to acknowledge the uneasy feeling that had been brought on by her conversation with Blaze. *I know he cares about me, but does he love me? I don't know.* Things had been great between them and Livi had smoothly settled into her role as his "wife."

Livi did not want to think about this right now. She just wanted to focus on work.

A few minutes later, Blaze appeared in the doorway of her office. "Hey, I thought we were supposed to have lunch together." His gaze was as soft as a caress.

Livi was surprised. "I totally forgot. I just had something to eat while I worked on the orders for the holiday season. Do you mind if we reschedule?"

He grinned. "You've been in the office one day and you're already rescheduling our lunch date."

"I'm sorry."

Blaze walked all the way into her office and said, "Honey, what's really going on? You look troubled about something."

She looked up, meeting his gaze. "I'm fine. It's just been a really busy day."

"Okay," he said, backing off.

She forced a smile. "Thanks."

Blaze stood there watching her.

Livi thought she detected a flicker in his intense eyes, sending her pulse racing alarmingly.

She loved Blaze beyond reason, but feared he did not feel the same way about her.

Livi gave herself a mental shake.

Surely, Blaze would not have wanted to stay married to her if he did not feel something for her. Not to mention that they were great together in and out of bed.

I'm worrying too much.

Livi silently chided herself for her insecurities.

They had agreed to take their relationship one day at a time, so she would just have to be patient with Blaze.

Saturday morning, Blaze and Livi drove to Pacific Palisades for another one of the Alexander family cookouts.

"What's on your mind, Livi?" he asked during the drive. "You're not your usual talkative self."

She glanced over at him. "It's nothing, really."

"Is it your new position?"

Livi smiled. "Partly. I'm making some headway, though."

Blaze reached over and took her by the hand. "Let me know if there's anything I can do to help."

His touch always warmed her to the core of her being. The loving look he gave her eased some of the apprehension she had been feeling over the past couple of days.

Livi allowed herself to relax.

Once they reached the Alexander estate, Blaze and

Ryan joined the men on the patio while Sage and Livi helped out in the kitchen.

Sage pulled out a bowl of tomatoes. She was about to make a garden salad.

Livi rinsed off the ears of corn, and then prepared to make homemade salsa.

"Have you and Blaze considered having a wedding ceremony?" Barbara asked. "To make your marriage legal."

"We haven't talked about a wedding," Livi responded. "I think that's a great idea."

"What's a great idea?" Blaze asked from the doorway of the kitchen.

"Your mother just asked if we considered having a wedding ceremony now."

He frowned. "Why would we need to do that?"

"Well, you don't really remember the first wedding," Barbara stated. "We could have a lovely ceremony, preferably in a church this time around."

Livi tried to read the expression on Blaze's face. He was clearly not thrilled with the idea of another wedding.

The apprehension she felt earlier was back.

Livi tried to shake it off.

"I don't think we have to do all that," Blaze uttered. "We're married. It's done."

"Your wife may not feel the same way," Sage interjected. "It's not all about you or what you want."

Blaze met Livi's gaze. "What do you think?" he asked her.

"I thought it was a wonderful idea."

He did not respond.

His reaction did not go unnoticed by Livi.

When he left the kitchen, Sage said, "Men…"

Livi gave a short laugh. "Apparently, one wedding was enough for Blaze."

"He'll come around," Barbara assured her. "I know my son."

Livi was not so sure.

Once Blaze made up his mind, there was no changing it.

"You've been awfully quiet most of the day," Livi observed aloud when they were preparing to drive back home. "What's wrong?"

"Nothing's wrong," Blaze responded. "I've just had a lot on my mind."

Livi did not press him.

Blaze was still in quiet mode when they arrived home. Livi had been preoccupied on the way there, but now it was Blaze who had nothing to say.

She sat down beside him on the sofa. "Please don't do this. Talk to me, sweetheart."

He looked over at her. "What do you want to talk about?"

"Why don't we start with what's bothering you, Blaze. I can tell that you're struggling with something. What is it?"

"Okay," he uttered. "Livi, I don't think we need to have a wedding. As far as I'm concerned, the first one did the trick."

His words pierced through Livi like a knife. "I see. But the thing is that we are not really married after all."

They stared at each other across a sudden ringing silence.

"What I meant is…"

She rose to her feet and walked to the window. "I'm pretty sure I know exactly what you meant, Blaze."

He followed her. "Livi, please hear me out."

Livi walked back to the sofa and sat down. She settled against the cushions with her arms folded across her chest. "I'm listening."

"I'm sorry, honey. I didn't mean to hurt you."

Livi shrugged in nonchalance. "Blaze, you don't have to apologize for being truthful. You don't want to marry me. I get it."

He released a soft sigh. "I'm not saying that I don't want to marry you, Livi. I just don't think we need to rush into it."

"I never would have moved in here, if I'd known that our marriage wasn't legal. I do not want to be your roommate, Blaze. I want to be your wife."

"Our wedding could become a media circus. I don't think either one of us wants to deal with that all over again."

"Blaze, I'm not looking to have some formal wedding with five hundred guests. I would prefer something much more intimate. Besides, this isn't about the media, is it? The truth is that you don't want to be tied down. You said that in the hospital in Las Vegas."

His mouth was tight and grim. "I care a great deal for you, Livi. I don't think I've ever been in love. People toss that word around so freely and I vowed never to do that. When I say those words, it's because I know it in my heart and soul."

"I guess I have my answer," Livi responded, "but what I don't understand is why you want to be in a loveless marriage. I don't get it."

"My mother reminded me of the sanctity of marriage. She wanted us to at least try to make this work."

"You did this for your mother? This was all about pleasing your mother? I can't believe this."

"Livi, you misunderstood."

She shook her head no. "I don't think so. I know how much you want to make your parents proud of you. I just never thought that included staying in a marriage that you did not want. I have been such a fool."

"Livi, please listen to me. I really wanted our marriage to work."

"There is no marriage and even if there was, it won't work without love, Blaze."

"We have been doing just fine, Livi." He sighed in resignation. "I don't even know how we came to be in this space."

"I saw your face when we were discussing another wedding ceremony. I saw it in your face, Blaze. You looked horrified at the thought of marrying me again." Livi blinked to keep her tears from falling.

"Things were great between us before we went to my parents' house this afternoon."

"No, they weren't," Livi said. "I've had this strange feeling that we were in different places for a few days now."

"You never said anything," he told her. "I thought we were supposed to talk things out—that's what we agreed to do."

"Blaze, we're talking now."

"Livi, I never saw myself married. It was not something I was planning on doing for a very long time, if ever. I truly wanted to make our relationship work and that hasn't changed."

"I want a man who loves me, Blaze. Someone who will love me as much as I love him."

"So where do we go from here?"

Chapter 21

Livi fought back her tears as her world began to crumble all around her. Sadly, it seemed that the best thing for them to do was to go their separate ways.

"I'm pretty sure it's time for me to move back to my own place," she said as casually as she could manage. Livi rose to her feet and walked toward the front door. "I need some air. I'm going out for a while."

"Now is not the time to run away, Livi."

She glanced over her shoulder. "I can't talk about this anymore. Not right now."

"Please don't leave, Livi."

She turned around to face Blaze. "What is it?"

"I don't want to give up on this marriage. I thought you didn't, either."

Livi swallowed hard, fighting back tears. Throwing a tantrum wouldn't help her now. She just needed to find someplace private to compose herself.

Livi was afraid that if she talked to Blaze now, she would fall apart. She did not want to give him the satisfaction of seeing that happen.

"Livi..." Blaze called after her.

"I have to get some air."

"It's raining," he said, but Livi did not slow her pace.

She took the elevator down to the lobby and rushed out into the rain. Walking onto Wilshire Boulevard, Livi felt as if she had been punched in the stomach. She wiped away her tears and walked briskly down the street. Rain poured, graciously hiding her tears. Using an old newspaper, she found on a nearby bench to shield her short hair, Livi stepped around a puddle of water. She made her way to the bookstore on the corner to wait out the downpour. She wiped her face with the back of her hand.

Running her fingers through rain-damp hair, Livi gazed upon row after row of bookshelves, a dark walnut color that gleamed under the store's fluorescent lighting. There were a handful of browsers, a couple of them holding books and other gift items.

She walked in the direction of the small café and ordered iced coffee. She found a chair and sat down. Each time her eyes landed on a couple, a flash of loneliness stabbed at her, icy fingers seeping into every pore of her being. A bitter-cold despair dwelt in the crevices of her lonely soul. Her heart ached terribly.

Livi tried to consider her options, but found that she was not in a space where she could wisely accomplish this. She thought about going back to her condo, but Sybil was still living there.

Livi pulled out her cell phone.

"Mother, I just called to let you know that I'll be

home tomorrow evening. I'm flying out in the morning."

She wiped away a tear. "No, I'm fine," Livi lied. "I just need to come home for a few days."

Livi stayed in the bookstore until the rain stopped.

She slowly made her way back to Blaze's condo.

Blaze was in his office. She walked straight to the master bedroom and pulled out a suitcase.

"What are you doing?" Blaze inquired when he entered the room.

"I'm packing," Livi responded. "I'm going to visit my parents for a few days."

"Livi, I don't want you to leave."

She glanced over at him. "I have to do this for myself. Blaze, I need to go somewhere where I can think about everything."

"I'm sorry."

"Stop apologizing," Livi snapped. "I don't want your apologies. Blaze, I don't want anything from you."

"I didn't want things to turn out like this. You wanted honesty and I gave you that."

"I can't talk about this right now, Blaze."

"Running away seems to be your answer to everything," he muttered.

"I can't believe that you just said that," Livi sniped.

"It's the truth."

"I am leaving because I need to think about what just happened in the last twenty-four hours. It's not as if I won't be back."

"If it's space that you need, Livi, I can stay at the hotel."

"This is your home, Blaze."

"It's also your home."

Livi shook her head no. "This has never been my home. All this has been one big beautiful lie."

"I'll have them get the jet ready for you."

"I'm going to drive, Blaze."

"You are not in the right frame of mind to drive, Livi." His tone brooked no argument. "You will have the family jet at your disposal."

"Thank you," she said softly.

"I really wish you wouldn't go."

She met his gaze. "Blaze, I need some time alone. Can you please give me that?"

"I don't have much of a choice, do I?" he responded.

Livi finished packing and then jumped into the shower. The jet was ready by the time she was dressed. Blaze insisted on driving her to the airport.

"Livi..."

She held up a hand to halt his words. "Don't, Blaze. We have both said enough for right now."

At the airport, Blaze embraced her and kissed her.

Livi did not respond. It was as if she were too numb to feel anything. She felt tired and weary. There was no more fight in her.

Blaze tossed and turned in bed most of the night. He was having a difficult time sleeping. He had grown used to sleeping beside Livi. Finally, he gave up and got out of bed. He padded barefoot into the living room and sat down in the dark.

Blaze had expected to hear from Livi upon her arrival, but she did not call him. When he tried calling her, he got her voice mail. Blaze thought about calling her again, but it was late and she was probably sleeping. He felt an ache in his heart. The memory of Livi's heartbroken expression and eyes filled with tears caused the pain to worsen.

Blaze missed everything about Livi. He could smell her fragrance lingering in the air. Whenever he walked into the kitchen, Blaze could almost hear her laughing and talking about her day as she prepared dinner.

His eyes grew wet.

Blaze walked into the family room and sat down. He picked up one of Livi's design magazines. He tossed it across the room.

Her presence had been felt and, now that she was gone, there was an emptiness that permeated the condo.

I miss her terribly. I don't want to lose her.

The thought of never seeing Livi again sent a new ache cutting through him like a knife. His heart felt as if there were a chunk missing. It was this ache that hurt the worst.

For a brief moment, Blaze considered going after her, but changed his mind. Maybe she needed some distance between them for now.

Blaze didn't feel like watching TV, so he got up and walked to his bedroom. He went to her side of the bed and picked up her pillow. He held it up to his nostrils, inhaling her scent.

Blaze dropped the pillow and walked briskly out of the room. He couldn't sleep there without Livi.

He stretched out on his sofa, but sleep was the last thing on his mind.

Upon her return, Blaze vowed to make up for all the pain he had caused Livi. He wanted her to know that he had been a fool. It had taken her leaving for him to realize that he loved her as much as she loved him. His whole soul pined for her.

Blaze had never felt the range of emotions for a woman that he was experiencing now. He would not feel complete until Livi was back in his arms.

Livi was glad to be in San Francisco. Shortly after her arrival, news broke that she was the heiress to Olson Cosmetics.

"It isn't as if it was never going to come out," her mother stated. "I don't know why you tried to hide your identity in the first place."

Livi shrugged nonchalantly. "I don't care anymore."

She sank down on the plush sofa in the family room. "Blaze shouldn't have to deal with all this alone. Have you spoken to him?"

Livi shook her head no. "Blaze has called me every day since I've been here," she said.

"Honey, from everything you've told me, it sounds like the two of you make a great team. I don't think you should just walk away from what the two of you share."

Livi met her mother's gaze. "Tell me something. Would you be as supportive if Blaze didn't have a cent to his name?"

She did not respond.

"I didn't think so," Livi said. "The only reason Blaze wanted to stay married to me was to please his parents. It was never about love."

"How do you know that for sure, Livi?"

She shrugged. "He said as much."

"Honey, make sure you're not being too hard on this man."

"I'm not," Livi stated. "I just don't want to keep fighting a losing battle."

Later that evening, Livi boarded the company jet to

return to Los Angeles. Blaze met her at the airport. He greeted her with a gentle kiss on the lips.

"I missed you," he said.

"I missed you, too," she responded.

"How was your trip?"

"Good," Livi responded. "I was able to think about everything."

"I did a lot of thinking, too," Blaze said.

"If you don't mind, I'd like to postpone any discussions until tomorrow. I'm really tired."

Blaze nodded. "Sure."

She walked into the condo thirty minutes later.

"I'm glad that you're home. If you'd like, I can sleep in the guestroom tonight," Blaze offered.

"I won't kick you out of your bedroom," she responded. "I'll sleep in the guestroom."

She did not miss the flash of disappointment on Blaze's face. This was not how she would have preferred to spend the evening, but Livi had no choice. Her dream of spending her life with Blaze had come true, but not exactly in the way she wanted.

Now she was left holding the pieces of her heart in her hands.

Chapter 22

Blaze could not escape the uneasy feeling he'd had since Livi's return. She was not the same woman he had spent the past few months with. Gone was that vibrant smile, and she was quiet—too quiet.

"If you're hungry, I can order something," he offered.

Livi shook her head. "I'm not hungry." She gestured toward the bedroom. "I think I'm just going to call it a night."

The forlorn expression on Livi's face said what her words did not.

She once believed in love and romance, but Blaze feared he had ripped all those things away from her.

Blaze wanted more than anything to put a smile back on her face.

The next day brought more of the same.

"I thought maybe we could have lunch together," he said, walking into Livi's office.

"I'm probably just going to order something in."

"Livi, I can't stand this distance between us," Blaze said, closing her door to give them some privacy.

"I'm going to be moving out this weekend," Livi announced without looking at him.

"That's not what I want."

"This isn't about you, Blaze. This is about me and what I want. I am not going to settle for living with you. I deserve better."

"We've been through a lot, Livi. Why do you want to give up now?"

"Because I think that I finally get the message." She looked at him. "Blaze, I don't think we're meant to be. We need to face the truth and just move on."

"Livi…"

"I really need to get back to work."

It was a curt dismissal.

That evening, Livi came home with boxes.

"Do you need any help?" he asked.

"No, I have it covered."

Blaze did not want her to leave, but he also could not force her to stay. He wanted to find a way to prove his love to her. It was the only way she would stay.

He had certainly made a huge mess of things.

I can't lose her.

Deep down, Blaze feared that he had already lost Livi, but he was not going to give up without one last fight for the woman he loved more than his own life. He had no idea when or how it happened, but Livi had captured his heart and soul.

* * *

Livi was surprised and bewildered by Blaze's reaction to her moving out. She had assumed he would be thrilled with the news, but he wasn't. In fact, quite the opposite.

She was not about to allow Blaze to unlock her heart. It was just too painful.

The last of her boxes on the moving truck, Livi glanced around the room one last time.

Blaze was in the living room when she walked out. "I really didn't think we would end up here," he said.

"Some things a relationship just can't survive," Livi murmured.

"That may be true, but we'll never know if ours can survive if we don't try. Sweetheart, please stay with me so that we can figure this out together."

"There's nothing to figure out," Livi responded. "You and I both know that it's not going to work."

"You don't want to try any longer?"

"Blaze, you are not in love with me," Livi stated. "I love you and I want to be loved in return. I won't negotiate on that."

"You deserve to be loved, and it wasn't until you left that it hit me. Honey, I do love you. I want us to be together."

Livi shook her head no. "You only think that you do. Blaze, you don't want a wife. I don't know what you want, but it isn't me."

"Okay, so I thought I wasn't ready to settle down. Can't you see that you've changed all that for me? Those days that you were gone were pure hell for me. I couldn't see you and I couldn't talk to you… Livi, I don't want you to leave."

"I'm not interested in living with you without marriage." Livi shook her head sadly.

"I thought you said you didn't ever give up without a fight."

"Even a fighter has to know when to walk away."

Livi had moved out two months ago and Blaze found he did not enjoy coming home to an empty house. It was one of the reasons he volunteered to fly to San Francisco to oversee the new marketing campaign. Blaze also found it awkward seeing Livi in the office when things were so tense between them. Her absence from his life ignited a gamut of emotions he had not expected. His feelings ran much deeper than Blaze had ever imagined.

He spent his time in meetings most of the day.

After his last meeting, Blaze called his father. "I'm coming home after Arizona," he announced.

"I think that's a wise decision, son."

"You knew how much Livi meant to me, didn't you?"

"I did," Malcolm confirmed. "But it wouldn't have mattered until you realized it yourself."

"Dad, I can't lose her."

"Then don't. In fact, come on home tonight. I can send someone to take over for you."

"Thanks, Dad."

Blaze headed straight to the airport. He was flying home to get Livi back. He was prepared to give Livi whatever she wanted. They belonged together and this time he was going to make sure it was forever.

Livi had heard that Blaze was going to be out of town for a couple of weeks. The thought of not seeing him saddened her. She had even heard talk that he was planning to relocate.

She would rather resign her position than have him walk away from the family business or move away because of her. Livi could not bear being the reason behind his departure. She still loved him, despite knowing that their relationship was over. In truth, it had been doomed from the start. Livi realized that now.

The knock on her door cut into her thoughts.

She gasped in surprise. "Blaze, I thought you were in San Francisco."

"I cut my trip short because I thought this was more important. May I come in?"

"Sure." Livi stepped aside to let him enter the condo.

"What's up?" she asked, her arms folded across her chest.

"As I told you before, I am not ready to give up on our marriage. I came over here to try to convince you to give me another chance."

"What we have is not a marriage, Blaze. It was all a lie."

"I don't believe that."

"Blaze, the only reason you were with me was because your mother wanted you to give the marriage a shot. It was not what you wanted."

"Maybe not in the beginning, but in the time we spent together, Livi, I fell in love with you."

She shook her head sadly. "It's too late, Blaze."

"Honey, it's never too late when it comes to love."

"Blaze, I can't do this dance again." Her eyes grew wet with tears. "I don't have any more illusions about us. I'm done."

"Do you still love me?" Blaze asked.

Livi did not respond. In fact, she did not look him directly in the eye, for fear he would see the truth.

"I know that you love me."

She remained silent.

"If you still love me, then give me another chance. Please."

Tears rolled down her cheeks. "I know that I wanted to give our marriage a shot, and I appreciate that you were willing to try, but we need to face the truth. This was never going to work. Just look at everything that happened."

"Livi, do you really think I would be trying this hard if I didn't want to be married to you?"

"I think this is more about your parents and what they want, Blaze."

He shook his head in denial. "That's not true."

Livi placed a hand to his cheek. "I think you had it right the first time. We should have gotten the marriage annulled. We are physically attracted to each other, but that was never enough to build a marriage on."

"So what are you telling me?"

"That what we had is over. It was never meant to be. I see that now."

Blaze sighed in resignation. "Are you sure that's what you want, Livi?"

"Yes." Pain ripped through her heart. She could not stop the tears from flowing. "It really is for the best. We tried Blaze. We tried and failed."

He shook his head. "I don't believe that."

The warmth of strong arms around her only made Livi's sobs louder.

"Shhh…sweetheart, it's going to be okay," he whispered, tears running down his own face. "Please don't cry."

Chapter 23

Blaze hated the sound of Livi's crying. It echoed his own breaking heart.

"Shhh..." he whispered.

Livi composed herself and tried to stand. Blaze wiped his own face, and then helped her up.

"I'll be right back," she said.

She washed her face and then returned to the family room where he was sitting. "I'm sorry for breaking down like that." Livi wouldn't look at him—she just stared down at her hands. She looked so lost and forlorn that Blaze yearned to pull her back into his arms.

"I don't agree that our marriage is over, but I can't work on it by myself," he told her. "If this is really what you want, then I have no choice but to respect your wishes."

"I can't be your friend, Blaze. My f-feelings are way too strong for that."

"I will always care for you, sweetheart."

She didn't respond.

Blaze rose to his feet. "Take care of yourself. Okay?"

Livi gave a slight nod.

"If you ever want to talk or if you need me, Livi… please don't hesitate to call."

"Goodbye, Blaze."

He resisted the urge to kiss her as he walked toward the front door. Blaze didn't have to look back to know Livi was crying. His heart broke all over again at the sound of her sobs. Blaze climbed into his car and drove away without looking back.

It took him a moment to realize that his face was wet from his own tears.

When Amy drove Livi back to the corporate offices after they had lunch together, Livi found Sage waiting for her.

Livi smiled. "Pregnancy certainly agrees with you."

"Thank you," she murmured.

Sage closed the door to Livi's office and then sank down in the visitor chair facing her. "I'll get straight to the point. I hate seeing you and Blaze like this. You haven't known my brother very long, but he is a good man and he's honest."

"I do know that about him," Livi stated.

"Blaze is very much in love with you. It just took him a little longer to realize it. He is heartsick over your breakup."

"I'm not happy about it, either," she confessed. "But it's for the best. I don't want to put myself or Blaze through a bunch of ups and downs."

"That's what marriage is about," Sage said. "Those ups and downs help you build character as a couple."

"I hadn't thought of it that way," Livi admitted.

"I hope you and Blaze will find your way back to each other." Sage rose to her feet. "You look as sad as he does."

Livi smiled. "Thank you for saying that, Sage."

The two women embraced.

"It's so good to see you." Livi pointed to Sage's round belly. "How's the little one?"

Sage broke into a wide grin. "*She* is doing quite well."

"It's a girl?"

"Yes. Ryan and I are thrilled to death. We both wanted a little girl."

Livi smiled. "That's wonderful. I'm so happy for you and Ryan."

"I hope that you plan on fulfilling your duties as auntie."

She was touched by Sage's words. "Of course."

Sage checked her watch. "I have a meeting in ten minutes. I'd better go make sure the room is set up as I requested. Blaze really is as miserable as you are," Sage said before she walked out of Livi's office.

"Livi's going to come around. Just give her some time," Barbara said. Blaze called his mother shortly after he arrived at work. He never called as much as he should, but he needed to talk to someone.

"Mom, she may still have feelings for me, but I don't think she's going to ever trust me again."

"Livi's hurting right now, but I have to believe that her love for you will bring her back," Barbara explained.

"Mom, I really messed up."

"Son, everyone makes mistakes. That's what life is all about. You have never been in love—not really. This is altogether different for you."

He gave a short laugh. "How could I just let Livi walk out of my life? I feel as if part of me is missing. I don't like feeling this way, Mom."

"Everything is going to work out, son. I have been praying for you and Livi and I know the good Lord is going to fix your marriage. Just have faith."

"I'm trying," he said.

"Don't give up on love. If what you have is real, then you and Livi will work through this situation."

Blaze talked for a few minutes more before ending the call.

"Knock, knock."

He looked up from his computer. "Sage, come in."

He was glad to see his sister, but had hoped to see Livi standing at his door.

"Blaze, I have never seen you this way." She sat down in the chair facing him. "I'm worried about you."

"I've never felt this way about anybody, Sage. I'm beginning to think that love is definitely not for me. I have all this emptiness inside."

"What are you doing to win your wife back?"

Blaze eyed his sister. "What can I do? She doesn't want anything to do with me. She will barely talk to me at work. I love Livi, but I don't think we have a future together."

"You don't if you don't talk to her and get this straightened out—that's for sure."

"That's just it. We can't resolve this, Sage. I don't

know what to do to make her believe that I love her and want to spend the rest of my life with her."

"Love is worth fighting for, Blaze. I can see how much pain you're in. I know that you love Livi and I know that she loves you just as much. How can you walk away?"

"Sage, it's not what I want. Trust me. I want Livi home with me. I want the life that we were trying to build together. I want to have children with her. I want all those things, but she doesn't believe me. What do I need to do to change that?"

"Show Livi that you love her enough to marry her all over again," Sage suggested.

Blaze shifted his position in his chair. "Have another wedding?"

"A real wedding ceremony, surrounded by family and vows you both will remember for the rest of your lives." She rose to her feet. "I need to get going. My job here is done."

Blaze got up and walked over to his sister, helping her out of the chair. "Thanks for the pep talk and the suggestion. I'm going to need your help pulling it all together."

She hugged him. "I love you, bro. Don't give up on Livi."

After Sage left his office, Blaze made a few more phone calls, including another one to his mother.

"Mom, how quickly can you plan a wedding?"

"When do you have in mind?" Barbara wanted to know.

"How about this weekend?"

"I'll make it happen."

"I'd like to have the ceremony on the beach at sunset."

When he finished his conversation, Blaze left his office to run some errands.

He ran into Livi in the hallway.

"I was just on my way to see you."

She gazed up at him. "About what?"

"I love you, Livi, and I'm not going to give up on you—not without a fight." Blaze took her by the hand and led her into his office, shutting the door behind them.

He pulled her close to him, kissing her passionately.

Livi responded, matching him kiss for kiss.

"I know that you still love me," he said.

"That doesn't mean that we should be together, Blaze."

He kissed her again. "Please don't do this, Livi. Don't walk out of my life. I know that I messed up and I'm sorry. Look, just give me this weekend. After this weekend, if you really want me out of your life, then I will accept your decision. I won't hold you back."

"Blaze, why do you want to drag this out?"

He met her gaze. "Because I love you. Trust me, I have never fought this hard for anything in my life, but you're worth it."

"You don't know how much I want to believe you."

"Livi, I won't ever let you down again. Just give me this weekend. I promise you that it will be rewarding."

She touched his cheek. "Please don't make promises that you can't keep."

"This has nothing to do with my parents," he said. "This is about what you and I want, and that's a life together."

"Can I think about it?"

He smiled. "As long as you give me an answer by

the end of the day. I'm going to be out of the office, but call me on my cell."

He kissed her. "I love you so much."

Livi hung to his words.

Chapter 24

Livi and Sybil left their Zumba class and headed down to the juice bar.

"So what are you going to do?" she asked Livi. "I know what I would do if I were in your shoes."

"My mind tells me to just move on with my life, but my heart… Sybil, I love him so much. But I don't know what to do."

"He must love you. I'm just saying…"

Livi took a sip of her smoothie. "I really want to believe that."

"From everything that you've told me about this man, I don't believe Blaze would be trying this hard if he didn't love you, Livi."

"His parents want us together. My parents want us together. I want to be with him. But the only question is this—what does Blaze really want? As long as that remains a question, we can't be together."

"Livi, I think you already have the answer to that question," Sybil stated. "Blaze may love his parents, but he strikes me as a man who makes his own decisions. You did say that he was the one who gave his parents the most problems growing up."

"But that's why he's trying so hard to make it work," Livi argued. "He wants to make up for the way he was when he was younger."

"That may be part of it, but it's not the whole deal. It never was, Livi." Sybil shook her head sadly. "You have a wonderful man who loves you and you are about to just kick him out of your life. Livi, I love you like a sister, but I have to be honest. You are about to make a huge mistake."

"Amy told me the same thing."

"Then what is wrong with you? Why aren't you going after your man?"

"Because we went about everything the wrong way," Livi said. "Our wedding vows were written on napkins, Sybil. Then, to top it off, we discover that we were never really married legally. The way I see it, we never had a good foundation to build on. Yes, I love Blaze, but that doesn't mean that we're meant to be together."

"It also doesn't mean that your marriage is not meant to be, either. Despite all that and the drama that followed, you two still want to be together. Livi, that should tell you something."

She met her best friend's gaze. "So you think I should give Blaze what he wants?"

Sybil nodded. "Definitely."

Livi waited until she got home to call Blaze.

He answered the phone on the second ring. "I didn't think I would hear from you."

"I needed to think about everything you said, Blaze," Livi responded.

"So what did you decide?" he asked.

"I'm going to give you this weekend. We'll try to see if we can make a go of this relationship."

Blaze released an audible sigh of relief. "Thank you, Livi. You won't regret it."

"Where are you taking me?" Livi asked when Blaze picked her up in a stretch limo.

He pulled out a strip of dark fabric. "It's a surprise."

Blaze blindfolded her.

"This might be considered kidnapping."

He laughed. "You are not being kidnapped."

"Then where are we going?" Livi asked a second time.

She reached out for his hand.

"Just relax and enjoy the ride," Blaze told her.

Livi leaned into his embrace. "I've missed you so much."

"I've been miserable without you," he confessed. "I haven't been able to sleep in my own bed because I can't forget what it felt like to make love to you there. You're in my blood."

The blindfold made Livi lose all sense of direction. She trusted Blaze with her life, but wasn't sure if she could trust him with her heart again.

"We're almost there," he told her before kissing her fully on the mouth.

Livi pulled his face back to hers. She savored the feel of his lips on hers. Loving him felt right, but she was scared. He had hurt her and she did not want to give him the chance to do it all over again. Yet, she could not resist spending the weekend with Blaze.

"Can I take the blindfold off?" she asked.

"Not yet," he said.

The limo pulled into a driveway and rolled to a stop.

Blaze helped Livi out of the car and removed the blindfold.

She looked around. "This is your parents' house. Why are we here?"

Livi did not know what to make of this situation. She swallowed her disappointment.

"Kellen and Zaire are in town," Blaze announced. "I thought it might be nice to spend some time with the family."

"That's fine." She pasted on a smile. It wasn't that Livi wasn't happy to see them, but she had thought that Blaze was whisking her off to some romantic getaway.

"Livi, it's so good to see you," Zaire said as she wrapped her arms around Livi. "I'm so glad you came."

"Same here," she responded with a smile. "Congratulations on receiving your MBA. Blaze told me that you've decided not to follow them into the family business."

"The Moore Group made me a phenomenal job offer and I just couldn't pass it up. I'm glad my parents are not upset about my defecting."

"Hey, pretty lady," Kellen said as he joined them.

Malcolm and Barbara were inside the house when they entered, followed by Zaire and Kellen.

Barbara embraced her first, and then Malcolm.

Blaze wasn't sure what he was going to say to Livi in front of his family, but he knew that it was time for him to make a move.

He embraced Livi, holding her tight.

Blaze inhaled deeply, sucking in the light floral scent of her perfume. “I brought you here because I’ve had a lot of time to think about our relationship and where we’re going with it.”

Livi nodded. “I figured as much.”

He led her over to the sofa in the living room. They sat down side by side.

“I want you to know that I love you with my whole heart.”

Her eyes grew wet with unshed tears. “Blaze, I love you, too, but…”

He put a finger to her lips.

“Livi, can you look me straight in my face and tell me that what we have shared is not worth fighting for? After all that we’ve been through?”

“At one time, I thought we had something, Blaze,” she responded. “Then I realized that you were not ready to be a husband. I do believe that you care for me, but I also feel that you don’t want to be tied down. I want to get married, Blaze. I want to have a family.”

“Livi, I don’t want to lose you,” Blaze said. “And that’s what this weekend is all about. I’m going to prove it to you.”

He kissed her.

“What we have is worth fighting for,” he whispered.

“I don’t know,” she responded softly. “Blaze, I’m tired. I can’t deal with the ups and downs that come with loving you. One minute we’re good and then things get crazy. I agreed to this weekend because I want to see if we have a chance at working things out, but I have to be honest. I don’t think we can because we don’t want the same things.”

"Honey, that's what being in a relationship is all about."

She met his gaze. "Blaze, you know that I love you. This is why it hurts so much. I thought I was married to the man of my dreams, but as it turns out, I wasn't. Finding out that our marriage wasn't real…that was the end."

"It's going to change, I promise you. Starting right now."

Blaze pulled out a tiny velvet box. "Livi, will you do me the honor of being my wife in every sense of the word?"

She gasped in surprise.

Livi's eyes bounced around the room. Barbara was smiling. Zaire had tears in her eyes, while Kellen and Malcolm stood there with grins on their faces.

Blaze had chosen a diamond-encrusted wedding band in platinum. "I just want you to know that I'm truly sorry for the pain I caused you. I would rather cut off my own hand before I ever hurt you again."

Livi wiped away her tears. "You really know how to surprise a girl."

"You still have not answered my question," he responded. "Will you marry me tomorrow evening at sunset?"

Livi gasped in surprise. "Tomorrow?"

Blaze nodded.

She gazed into his eyes and saw the love reflected there. He loved her and he wanted to marry her all over again. "You really want this?"

"More than anything else in the world," Blaze responded with a grin. "I can't see my life without you in it."

Livi glanced down at the ring he was about to place

on her finger. "Blaze, I would be honored to marry you tomorrow at sunset."

Zaire squealed and began jumping up and down.

Kellen pulled out his cell phone and called Ari. "She said yes. Tell the rest of the clan that we're having a wedding tomorrow."

Livi laughed. "When did you plan all this?"

Blaze glanced over at his mother. "She's the one who pulled everything together."

Franklin entered the room carrying a bottle of champagne. "I hear we're having a wedding this weekend."

Livi hugged him. "Yes, we are."

Barbara prepared a celebratory lunch for them.

Afterward, Blaze and Livi walked down to one of the villas. "We're staying in a guesthouse because I wanted some alone time with my wife-to-be."

Livi was giddy with happiness.

Exchanging their vows before friends and family would be a wonderful way to begin their life truly as husband and wife. Livi no longer had any doubts about Blaze. She was free to love him with her whole heart.

Inside the villa, they sat down to talk.

Blaze kissed her instead.

Livi responded by kissing him back passionately. Desire ignited in the pit of her belly, the flames growing.

Blaze struggled against the urge to take Livi into the bedroom and make love to her. He wanted to wait until their wedding night, and had not planned to stay in the villa with her until after the ceremony.

She must have sensed his withdrawal, because Livi moved away from him. "Blaze, is something wrong?"

He shook his head no. "I want to wait until after

we exchange vows before making love to you. Zaire is going to stay with you in the villa tonight."

She laughed. "I was actually thinking the same thing. I wanted to wait until we had the wedding."

"You have made me a very happy man," Blaze told Livi. "This time it's forever."

Livi agreed. "I just don't want any shadows lingering across our hearts. If you have any, then we do not need to go through with another wedding."

"My heart is clear," he responded. "I am certain that I want to spend the rest of my life with you and I want you to be the mother of my children."

Livi broke into a grin. "Babies."

"Yeah…lots of babies."

"How many?" she wanted to know.

"As many as we want."

Zaire threw an impromptu bridal shower for Livi. They sat around in the living room of the villa, eating and playing shower games. Livi had never laughed so hard. Her sides were hurting. The Alexander women certainly knew how to let their hair down.

"Okay, ladies, it's time for the gifts," Zaire announced. "Now, as you know, this is a lingerie shower, so I hope y'all didn't come here with some towels or a toaster."

Sybil thrust a gift-wrapped package toward Livi. "Open mine first."

"When did you have time to buy a gift? Did you know what Blaze had planned?"

She nodded with a smile. "He called us to let us know."

Livi opened her gift and gasped. "Only you would

buy me something like this." She held up the barely there teddy. "This looks like it might hurt in all the wrong places."

Zaire took it from her and said, "Hey, if you're not going to use it..."

Behind them, Barbara cleared her throat loudly.

"Mama, please tell me you didn't hear that," Zaire said, embarrassed.

Barbara smiled warmly and responded, "Oh, I have a couple of those in my dresser."

Sage almost choked on her lemonade. "Mama...I really did not need to know that."

Livi cracked up with laughter.

They spent the rest of the evening laughing and talking about the ups and downs of marriage. Zaire, on the other hand, talked about being single but looking forward to finding a husband.

Natasha could not keep her eyes open, so she stretched out on the sofa and fell asleep while the others watched a movie.

Ari came down to get her, but did not wake her. He planted a kiss on her cheek and left.

Sage stayed, as well. She called Ryan to let him know they were having a slumber party.

Barbara rode back to the house with Ari.

"I can't believe this is really happening," Livi confided to Sybil. "I had no idea that Blaze was going to propose. He completely surprised me."

"I'm so glad you and Blaze have decided to make it official. I also always thought he was the one for you."

"So did I," Livi said. "I felt that we were meant to be together."

She picked up a pillow and held it close to her. "I

never imagined that I could be so excited about marrying a man I thought I was already married to—it's crazy."

"It's just that you two are finally on the same page," Amy interjected.

"It certainly took us long enough."

Chapter 25

While the women were all down at the villa with Livi, Blaze and his brothers sat out on the patio talking.

"Blaze, I have to tell you that I never, ever thought you would be getting married," Kellen announced. "I figured you would be the last of us getting hitched, if ever."

Ari laughed. "I'm with you, Kell. I never thought he'd turn in his player card, either."

Blaze laughed. "Hey, when you meet that certain someone, things change."

Ari and Ryan agreed.

"I never thought any woman could mean so much to a man. I felt as if I couldn't breathe when she told me that she wanted to move out."

Kellen chuckled. "She had my brother all choked up. I called to check on him, and Blaze couldn't talk. Sounded to me like he'd been crying."

"I wouldn't say that," Blaze said. "But I was hurt by the breakup."

"Oh, I would," Ari interjected. "Man, you were all broke down. You couldn't eat or sleep."

"The way you were when you thought you'd lost Natasha," Blaze countered.

Ari pointed at Ryan. "I know you're not laughing. Before you left for New York, I thought we were going to have to put you out of your misery. You were one sad puppy."

Ryan nodded in agreement. "I don't know how we let these women get under our skin like that. They can wound a brotha deeply."

They all nodded in agreement.

"But they love just as deeply," Ari said.

Blaze agreed. "Livi is something else when you cross her, but it's one of the things I love about her."

"I can say the same thing about Sage. One minute she's ready to bite my head off, but she is just as passionate in everything she does."

"I wasn't sure where you were going with that," Kellen said. "Some things I don't need to know about my sister."

They laughed.

"What do you think they're doing?" Ryan inquired.

"My wife is sleeping," Ari stated. "The others were sitting around watching a movie."

Blaze released a long sigh. "I can't wait until tomorrow evening. I miss Livi."

Kellen put a finger to his lips. "Shhh…you're about to lose your man card. Don't ever say that again and particularly with such feeling."

Everyone laughed.

"Kellen, you just wait. Some girl is going to have you groveling at her feet. Trust me."

He shook his head no. "Not me. I'm way too cool for that."

"I used to say the same thing," Blaze replied. "I'm telling you, when you meet the right one, things change. You change."

"Man, you need to go on down to the villa with the girls," Kellen said with a grin. "You don't even sound like my brother."

"What's going on?" Livi asked Blaze the next morning when she went up to the main house. "Where is everybody?"

"Checking on our wedding plans."

"I need to run out and find something to wear," Livi announced. "It just hit me this morning that we are actually getting married in a few hours."

"Everything's been arranged," he assured her. "Our clothing, the wedding ceremony, the dinner after and even our honeymoon. I don't want you worrying about anything."

"Your mother did all this in such a short time. That's incredible."

"She had the help of a wedding planner."

"How did you know I was going to agree to this?"

He stared in her eyes. "Because you love me as much as I love you. We both want the same thing and that's to be together."

Blaze pulled her into his arms, kissing her.

"Enough of that," Sage said as she and Ryan walked into the room. "We have a lot to do before the wedding. First, we need to make sure your dress fits. Martha is at the boutique and she's expecting us. I had it delivered to her."

"Who picked it out?" Livi asked.

"I did," Sage answered. "I'm pretty sure you're going to love it. It's absolutely beautiful."

"After we pick up your dress, we will meet Mom and the others at the spa," Sage announced. "Blaze and the men will be doing whatever they need to do for the wedding."

"This is really happening," Livi murmured softly.

Blaze planted a kiss on her forehead. "I'll see you at sunset. I'll be the man standing with the pastor beneath the arches."

"I'll see you there," she said with a grin.

Livi had not been able to see the setup for their ceremony because Blaze wanted to surprise her with every aspect of their wedding. He did tell Livi that they were writing their own vows, however.

She enjoyed the creativity Blaze employed to make their wedding memorable. Filled with anticipation, Livi was looking forward to the evening.

Shortly before sunset, the Alexander family and their invited guests gathered on the beach.

A Balinese-style umbrella had been fashioned at the entrance of the walkway that led down to the beach. There was a bamboo arch decorated with flowing drapes of silk and organza in vibrant oranges and reds. Floral arrangements of calla lilies adorned the makeshift altar. Tiki torches accented with organza ties, silk ferns, flowers and sea grass decorated the aisle. Three classical musicians played romantic selections as they waited for the arrival of the bride.

* * *

Wearing a fitted white lace gown with a red-and-orange taffeta sash that also served as the train, Livi stood in the middle of the bedroom. Amy secured her headpiece made of pearls, charms and rhinestones, which had both a vintage and ultramodern feel. Livi wore her short, curly hair slicked back.

"I just went down to the beach and everything looks great," Zaire announced. "My brother really did a good job. I noticed some news helicopters flying overhead. I'm sure we have a few uninvited guests lurking somewhere."

"I'm not going to let them ruin this day for me," Livi said with a shrug of nonchalance. "I don't care what they report."

Livi checked her watch. "It's almost time for the ceremony to begin. We need to head down."

Zaire left the room, leaving Livi alone with her best friends.

"I never thought this day would come," she told Sybil. "Blaze and I are getting married…well, getting married officially. I don't think either one of us remembers what we said the first time around."

"This one will be more meaningful for you both," Amy commented. "I'm so happy for you."

Livi agreed.

"You look beautiful."

"So do you, Sybil." Livi picked up her bouquet of calla lilies. "Everything is perfect…well, almost. I just wish my parents could be here. This will be the second wedding I've had that they have missed."

"You weren't able to reach them?"

Livi shook her head no. "It's not like them not to return my calls. I guess my dad must have had a game today and Mom went with him."

"C'mon, Livi," Amy told her. "Time to walk into your future with the man you love."

They left the bedroom.

Livi gasped in surprise when she saw her parents standing at the foot of the stairs.

Her eyes filled with tears of happiness. "What are you two doing here? I kept trying to call you."

"Blaze called us last night and told us about the wedding," her father said. "They sent the corporate jet for us, so that we could be here."

Livi's mother pulled out a tissue and dabbed at her daughter's eyes. "Don't ruin your makeup, sweetie." In a low voice, she whispered, "These people have a lot of class. I think we are going to be one big happy family."

The two women embraced. "I'm so glad you and Daddy are here. Now my day is absolutely perfect."

Outside the house, Kellen was waiting to escort her mother down to the beach and to her seat.

Livi and her father followed behind Amy and Sybil, her maids of honor.

Zaire was right. Blaze had done a great job making sure that her tastes were reflected in their wedding, such as her favorite colors, which were red and orange with undertones of eggplant and deep plum. Livi described the palette as the colors of sunset.

Livi's father kissed her cheek before escorting her down to the altar.

He placed her hand in Blaze's hand and said, "I expect you to take good care of my daughter."

Blaze said his vows first. "Livi, I take you to be my wife. I want you to know that I will always cherish you and your love. I will never take you for granted. I will trust and respect you, be faithful to you and love you until the end of my life. Even then, I will love you throughout eternity. I give you my heart, and my love, from this day forward for as long as we both shall live."

Livi smiled through her tears. "The vows we made the first time around were beautiful, but they do not come close to what you just said. Blaze, I love you. I want you to be my best friend, my lover and the father of my children. We have waited two long years to get to this moment, and I want you to know that I am looking forward to growing old with you. I promise to love and cherish you through whatever life may bring us. These things I give to you today, and all the days of our life."

Livi could hardly contain her excitement as she waited to hear the words that would make their union real to her.

"I now pronounce you husband and wife…"

Blaze exhaled a long sigh of pleasure. He pulled Livi into his arms, drawing her close. He pressed his lips to hers for a chaste, yet meaningful kiss.

His eyes traveled down the length of her, nodding in obvious approval. "You look so beautiful, sweetheart. I love you, Mrs. Alexander."

"I love you, too, Mr. Alexander."

Livi held up her hand to admire her wedding ring. "It didn't feel real the first time around. This time feels different, though."

Blaze agreed. "I feel the same away."

The photographer that Blaze hired took pictures of them alone and with family.

Afterward, they headed up to the Alexander estate for a poolside reception.

The patio had been transformed into a tropical paradise for the evening. Tall, clear vases filled with water and a variety of fruits, orchids and tulips made visually stunning centerpieces. Floating candles in the pool illuminated the water. Glass tables with chairs were arranged around the pool where guests could sit.

Rattan baskets of flip-flops and pool towels in the wedding colors were stationed around the patio for guests to choose and take home as wedding favors.

The musicians took their place near the fireplace and prepared to treat the guests to more soft, romantic music, designed to accentuate the calming feel of the pool area and the beauty of the evening.

Livi smiled at Blaze. "Everything is perfect."

"I wanted our wedding to be a reflection of us."

"Romantic, intimate and small," she murmured. "It truly is everything I wanted, Blaze. Thank you." Livi turned to face him. "Flying my parents in to share this evening with us was the best gift you could have given me."

"I have something else for you," Blaze said.

"What?"

He picked up a box from a nearby table and handed it to Livi.

"Sneakers!" she said with a laugh. Livi loved the sequined white tennis shoes and immediately slipped them on her feet.

"You always complain about having to take your shoes off for dancing, so I thought I'd get you these so that we can dance the night away."

"I love them," Livi murmured. "They even say *bride* on the label. These are too cute. We are going to have to get some of these for the boutique."

Their conversation died with Harold DePaul's sudden appearance.

"I came to offer my congratulations to the bride and groom," he said. Holding up a gift-wrapped box, Harold asked, "Where do I put this?"

"Thank you for your thoughtfulness," Livi said, taking the gift from him.

"I've always liked you and…well, I'm happy for you. Blaze is a good man and I'm sure he will make you very happy." Harold glanced around. "I just stopped by to drop off the gift. I didn't see my sister earlier or I would have sent it with her."

"Harold, you don't have to leave," Blaze blurted out. "This is a family celebration and you *are* family."

"Are you sure you want me to stay?" he asked.

Livi linked her arm through his. "Of course we do, Harold. It is time for you to get to know Blaze and his family. Really get to know them."

Malcolm invited Harold to sit at their table.

"I think he's finally coming around," Livi whispered to Blaze.

"I'm not as convinced, but I'm willing to give the man a chance."

Livi placed a hand on his cheek. "This is one of the reasons I love you."

Meredith walked over and said, "I told Harold about the ceremony, so it's my fault that he's here."

"It's fine," Blaze assured her. "We weren't trying to keep it a secret. Besides, I think someone on staff may have alerted the press. Rumors started circulating on the internet yesterday as to why Livi and I were getting married again."

"Really?" Livi uttered. "What are they saying?"

"It doesn't matter," he responded. "This night is about us, so let's get this party started."

The DJ took to the microphone.

Blaze and Livi got up to dance. Instead of the traditional slow dance, they decided to show off their moves to Beyoncé's latest hit. Sage and Ryan, Zaire and Kellen joined them.

Not to be outdone, Livi's parents got up and made their way to the dance floor, followed by Malcolm and Barbara.

Amy took Harold by the hand and led him to the dance floor.

"Instead of tossing the bouquet and the garter belt, we decided to do something different," Blaze announced later in the evening. "We had the single ladies sit at certain tables and the same with the men. If you would look under your chair, there is a red rose taped to one of them."

Zaire squealed. "I have it. I have the rose."

Laughing, Livi handed the bouquet to her.

Blaze threw back his head and laughed at the expression on Franklin's face when he pulled a rose from under his chair.

"This has been so much fun," Zaire said as she hugged her sister-in-law.

"Yes, it has," Livi agreed. "It looks like everyone is having a good time, including Harold."

"Your wedding has been as special as you and Blaze. This is what I want when I get married—a wedding that mirrors my personality. Of course, I have to find a husband first."

"You won't have a problem with that, Zaire."

"I don't know. I'm not doing that great in the boyfriend department."

"This is how it usually works for most people, I think. I was pretty much done with dating when I met your brother. However, the time we spent together in Las Vegas changed all that for me. Those three days unexpectedly turned into a five-star romance. Just remember that sometimes an impulsive act can turn into forever."

* * * * *